where
the
light
falls

Gretchen Shirm worked as a lawyer for over ten years. Her first book *Having Cried Wolf* (2010) was shortlisted for the UTS/Glenda Adams Award for New Writing. She was named as a 2011 *Sydney Morning Herald* Best Young Australian Novelist. Her fiction, criticism and non-fiction has been published in *The Saturday Paper*, *Best Australian Stories*, *Australian Book Review*, *The Australian*, *The Monthly*, *Art Monthly*, *The Sydney Morning Herald*, *Review of Australian Fiction* and *Southerly*.

www.gretchenshirm.com

Praise for *Having Cried Wolf*
'*This collection is beautifully formed.*'

The Age

'*A major new talent has arrived.*'

Kerryn Goldsworthy, *Sydney Morning Herald*
'*Wintonesque.*'

Sunday Herald Sun

'*Deep emotional truths.*'

Canberra Times

'*You're in the hands of a born storyteller . . .*'

Cate Kennedy

where the light falls

GRETCHEN SHIRM

ALLEN&UNWIN
SYDNEY・MELBOURNE・AUCKLAND・LONDON

First published in 2016

Copyright © Gretchen Shirm 2016

Allen & Unwin
83 Alexander Street
Crows Nest NSW 2065
Australia
Phone: (61 2) 8425 0100
Email: info@allenandunwin.com
Web: www.allenandunwin.com

Cataloguing-in-Publication details are available
from the National Library of Australia
www.trove.nla.gov.au

ISBN 978 1 76011 365 0

Set in 12.5/18 pt Bembo by Post Pre-press Group, Australia
Printed and bound in Australia by Griffin Press

10 9 8 7 6 5 4 3 2 1

The paper in this book is FSC® certified.
FSC® promotes environmentally responsible,
socially beneficial and economically viable
management of the world's forests.

Art is not about art. Art is about life.

LOUISE BOURGEOIS

1

In winter, the dark was terrible. He walked into his apartment at six and already it was pulled down over the city like a hood. The night had a texture, a thick woven fabric, fine as knitted wool. He could never have imagined it: a darkness more bitter than the cold. When he came home at night, he pressed the door of his apartment closed, aware each time that he was performing an act of resistance against it.

Inside their apartment, the light slanted upwards from lamps and bare bulbs. The wiring in the walls was old and the lights in the ceilings did not work. Still, it felt welcoming. It gave the room a staged effect. Moving through their apartment was like walking through a theatre production; the light threw his shadow in different directions and as he passed a lamp, his shadow jumped on a wall, crooked and threatening.

It was always a relief, this moment of returning home, of settling back into himself after a day at work in his studio. An hour later, Dominique walked in wearing a woollen cloche hat. It was a crimson hat that she often wore in winter, its colour a cry of protest in the grey Berlin streets. She pushed her hair up beneath it and it kept her warm that way she said, because no cold air could sneak up inside it. She moved with the appearance of gliding.

That night she cooked a Spanish omelette, large and yellow in the pan like the face of a sun, and he prepared the salad, removing the outer leaves from the lettuce, dismantling the heart and chopping the vegetables into strips. Dom poured the wine into two glasses big enough for soup.

The next day was Dom's last in Berlin before she left for Cologne for two weeks. She was teaching contemporary dance to a promising group of teenagers. When he saw her with her students, he admired the way she spoke to them, as though they were no less than her, that their love of dance made them equal.

Dom no longer danced professionally. He'd heard it said that a dancer dies two deaths, and her first death had occurred before they'd even met. When she spoke about it, he saw the wound it had caused inside her, the sadness she felt at never having quite got the break she wanted. He admired her ability to speak so openly about failure.

He'd seen footage of her, a film made of her last solo performance for a small company in Hamburg. She moved on stage as though possessed of another force and, at that moment, she was preoccupied only with her movements, her eyes open and her face clouded not with concentration, but with strain of the physical effort. He had seen the same look on her face when they were in bed together; as if she were searching for something inside herself that was just beyond her grasp. He had watched that film more times than he could count.

He couldn't help but think that the dancer he saw was different to the woman he loved—now her features bore the trace of a wound, the knowledge of defeat. He loved her because of rather than in spite of that. She had found the limit of her own ability, which most people never had the courage to reach.

That night, before he went to bed, he checked his email. He had an exhibition coming up in London and he was still in the process of making new work. Models had to be found, photographic assistants hired for his shoots and props and equipment located. The exhibition was only six weeks away and no matter how early he began his preparations, the lead-up to a new show was always hectic. But there was nothing about the exhibition in his inbox.

Instead, there was a message from his old friend Stewart Carey. He saw the name and an old life beckoned him. Stewart and he had been at high school together and Stewart was the only person from that former life whom Andrew kept in touch with. The subject line read: *Kirsten*. This name, too, belonged to a past life, a version of himself he had tried to leave behind when he'd moved to Berlin three years ago.

Hi Andrew,

I'm not sure if you heard, but just in case you haven't, I thought you would want to know. Kirsten Rothwell is missing. It's been three weeks now. They found her car beside Lake George. Sorry to tell you this way, mate.

I hope things are going well in Berlin. Call if you get some time. Say 'hi' to Dom from us.

Stewart

Andrew read the message through twice. His eyes skipped over the words as if by reading them quickly he could reduce their impact. But it was too late. *Missing*, he thought. Perhaps that meant she simply didn't want to be found. With Kirsten, something like that had always seemed possible. Maybe she had decided she needed some time away from the world. And yet there was a finality to Stewart's tone; was he hinting at something more definite? He had the feeling as he read the words again of their immensity; he knew they meant much more to him than he was currently able to grasp.

He stood from his chair and his heart was beating fast, throbbing in a strange rhythm.

'Are you okay?' Dom asked.

'I—I just received some bad news.'

'What happened?' Dom said, concerned. She looked up from the book she was reading.

He looked at her and he did not want to tell her.

'I just—I got an email from Stewart.' She took his hand as he spoke and he saw it was shaking. 'About a friend. An old friend of mine who I knew when I was at university. She's missing.'

'Oh no. What happened?' Dom was looking at him with clear eyes, willing to absorb some of the hurt he felt.

He had no words to explain it. His reaction to the news wasn't even one of sadness, but shock. He walked to the kitchen and poured himself a glass of water, which he drank in a few, quick gulps.

'I don't know exactly. Stewart didn't say much.' He moved from their kitchen to the living room and sat down at their table. In front of him was a pile of opened mail. 'Just that she's been missing now for almost three weeks.'

On the wall of their apartment, he'd pinned an unframed photo he'd taken a few weeks before: the face of a young boy, looking up and smiling with his eyes closed. It was for his upcoming exhibition. It was an important exhibition for him—his first solo show in London—and he was running out of time to make new work. He hadn't been able to think of a title for that image, but now the words *Smiling Alone* occurred to him. He'd asked the boy to smile that way, with his teeth visible, but sitting there with this new information yet to settle inside him, the image suddenly looked terrifying. The boy's second teeth had just come through and they were still jagged and yet to be worn down to a smooth edge.

'Were you close to this woman?' Dom asked. She ran a finger along his cheek in an upwards stroke. Her face was close to his and open to whatever his answer might be.

'We were, I suppose, while I was at art college. But I haven't spoken to her since I moved to Berlin.' He didn't want to disclose to Dom that he had once loved this woman or that he had let it continue between them for longer than he should have. He didn't want Dom to know that the reason he had fled Sydney, in the end, was to escape her.

2

The next morning was a Sunday and they woke slowly, waking and sleeping and waking again. They had bought the bedsheets together the week before; they were still stiff and folded around their bodies in pleats. Dom slipped out of bed first and made them coffee on the stove with the small espresso jug that fizzled as the water percolated. He watched her against the background of their kitchen, the white glow of the cupboards on her face.

As she walked back to bed the floorboards gave under her feet with small clicks, the friction of wood against wood. She walked with her feet turned out and he loved the fact that dancing had permanently shaped her. Her body was sinuous and firm, still refusing to relinquish the strength that dancing had given it. Her breasts were the only part of her that was soft, her nipples large and mauve on her brown skin. Along her arms and shoulders, a dusting of freckles dispersed across her skin, speckled like a bird's egg.

She stretched on the floor while he drank his coffee in bed; she could still bend her body along her legs easily, folding herself in half like a soft doll to grasp her feet with her hands. In the middle of winter she cursed when her muscles tightened and she couldn't sit on the ground in the splits.

Watching her, he understood; was it for the first time? Or did the realisation grow, coming to him gradually, the words repeated in his head until it slowly became something he knew? He'd never thought it possible, to have this feeling of being in love without also feeling that he was also losing part of himself.

She came back to bed and spooned him, her skin cold against his warmth. She had done this often at night when he lay awake, worrying. Lately that was often. He was thirty-seven and his existence was still precarious; he lived from exhibition to exhibition. The basic anxiety about whether he would make enough money to survive was constant, although there was more of a market for his work in Europe and his income more reliable since he moved to Berlin. On those nights when he couldn't sleep, Dom talked him through his fears, reassuring him that, no matter what, they would find a way through. She was more generous to him than he'd ever been to himself.

The upcoming show in London was causing him many sleepless nights. He still needed one standout photograph, an image that would make people take notice, and would bring him the important acquisition of his work he needed. He was so desperate for this exhibition to be a success that he was sure it was bound to end in failure. Things had gone badly before—he'd had exhibitions from which he hadn't sold a single print—but if this show didn't succeed he would have to reckon with failure at a whole new level. London was an important market and this was his first real break after almost a decade of trying.

For many years in his life, he'd only had to worry about disappointing himself, but now, with Dom in his life, the stakes were much higher than they'd been before. Maybe he felt he could only expect her to love him when things were going well, that the successful version of him was worthy of love, but the failure would never be.

Andrew rolled over and he was so close to Dom's face that he could see the freckles on her nose, diffuse and delicate, although her skin was dark. Her father, whom he'd met many times, had migrated to Germany from Ghana before she was born, although her mother was born in Bremen and her skin was a bluish white. Dom was a combination of the two.

He pulled the sheet up over them as they lay together and the light around them was gauzy and white.

'Did you sleep okay last night?' she asked, looking up at him. His arms were around her, one under her neck. Her body flush against his. When they lay together like this, he sometimes thought he could feel the faint throb of her heart through her skin. But perhaps it was only his own.

'Okay,' he said.

'You got up at one point and turned on the light?'

He nodded. 'Yes, I couldn't switch my mind off.'

'Were you worrying about the exhibition in London again?'

'No, it wasn't that.'

In truth he had been thinking about Kirsten, fighting off memories from the past that had no place here, in his life with Dom. But the more he tried to banish those thoughts, the more intrusive they became. There was something about his relationship with Kirsten that felt unresolved. In the years before he left Sydney, she had seemed increasingly troubled. Still he'd kept seeing her; he felt he couldn't stop. Kirsten was more addiction than attachment. In the end, the only way to free himself from her was to leave Sydney, to cut her from his life. But he had been too afraid of hurting her to tell her this directly.

'I was thinking about the friend from Sydney who went missing. There was something about Stewart's email that made me think it must be serious. I don't think he'd bother to contact me otherwise. I'm sorry I woke you.'

'Don't be sorry,' she said and she pulled herself away a little, still looking into his face, as though this distance would help him too see how much she empathised with his concerns.

•

They rose and slipped into their jeans and took their heavy coats from the hangers. The fabric of his coat was stiff from being worn for too many winters and the material hung heavily from his body like the skin of a bear. They walked hand in hand to the café around the corner and slipped onto a bench seat, sitting side by side, their thighs pressed together. Over breakfast they hardly spoke. Their best exchanges, he often thought, were wordless, when all they shared between them was a mood. Dom sat absorbed in *Die Welt* while he flicked through *Der Spiegel*, seeking out the few articles in English. He ordered muesli and it arrived with gooseberries on top and they burst between his teeth, their flavour bright and unusual.

Afterwards, they walked through Mitte together, down Alte Schönhauser Allee, drifting in and out of shops, the same shops they always went into, a path they often took, following a set of footprints they had laid many times before. Around him were the familiar fixtures of concrete, a landscape of grey with sudden eruptions of graffiti on the walls. These streets and lanes had become familiar to him, a pattern that now held a shape in his brain and he walked through this area with the feeling that he belonged.

•

That night they went to the exhibition opening of a friend of his. Outside the cold had turned sharp. The severity of winter was always a shock, a long dark tunnel of black nights and scantly lit days. He reminded himself that it was the last day of January and in a month winter would start to lift.

They took the U-Bahn to Rosa-Luxemburg-Platz, walked past the Volksbühne theatre and the Babylon cinema, and waited on the street to be buzzed into the gallery. He looked down through the lower window and saw people already milling in the basement. The light was orange and sparse, as though the room was lit by embers. Berlin was a place in which you needed to know the right doors to pass through and it came as a sudden surprise, standing there, to find himself in a position of knowledge.

Inside the gallery, Dom stood in front of him with her back pressed against his chest. The colour was the first thing he noticed about the paintings, thick reds, oranges and browns, autumnal colours across the canvas, warm but with the sense of approaching darkness. The images started to take shape, landscapes, loosely formed hills and trees, and the colours made them look burnt. They were scenes of a world that was ending.

They moved between the canvases and other people in the gallery turned and looked towards them. He began to wonder if they were standing too close to the work, or moving against the current of people. It took him some time to understand that there was a sort of jealousy about their gaze, that Dom and he shared something between them that these people envied. There are occasional moments when you love someone and you are aware of it, and there in the gallery he felt that small, bright miracle taking place between them.

But then their friends arrived—some were people Dom knew, others had studios in the same building as his—and the awareness passed, moving off behind him and into his wake. They stayed and drank and talked. No-one felt they needed to say anything complicated or profound. They spoke of things they had spoken of before and would speak of again. There was a simplicity to their conversation, a warmth and an ease.

When they left the gallery a rain had started, icy wet drops that weren't quite snow, falling on the ground around them with a lisp, *thsst, thsst, thsst*. Later, in bed, they slept naked together, sharing the warmth of their bodies against the chill of winter that was slipping through the gaps in the blankets.

•

The next morning, he drove Dom to the Hauptbahnhof in the old car she'd had since she was twenty-five. It was a small car and they sat with their knees pressed up against the dashboard. They were quiet together. In these moments after waking, his thoughts took some time to catch up to his movements.

It was 7 am and Berlin was still dark, the streets empty. He didn't park at the train station, but dropped Dom at the entrance. She leant across to kiss him and her mouth was warm on his.

'The next two weeks will be a bit full on, but I'll call you whenever I can,' she said, extracting herself from the small car.

As he drove away he watched her in the rear-view mirror as she wheeled her bag into the station, until she got smaller and he turned out onto the autobahn and could no longer see her.

•

He drove straight to his studio in Mitte. The large room was still and cold. He turned on the heating and sat down with his back to the wall, listening to the trickle of oil. He stayed there for what must have been an hour, but his mind was no longer on Dom and Berlin. He was thinking about Kirsten and Sydney. He had been born in Sydney and had lived there for most of his life, but he hadn't been back to visit in almost two years, not since his last exhibition. He hadn't seen his mother in as long.

It was a city that belonged to a different era of his life, a period of struggle. It was a time in his life characterised more by failure than by success, when he woke each morning and told himself, *Keep going.* Those were the words he repeated to himself in the face of every adversity, of failures and setbacks that would have caused most people to quit.

There were successes. Enough at least, to make him persevere—the sale of his work to important institutions, grants to fund the making of new work—but the more success he had, the more the rejections burned. Five years ago, an influential gallery in Melbourne had scheduled an exhibition of his work, but when they saw the photographs he'd taken, they politely declined to show them. It was the greatest disappointment of his artistic career, the only moment he'd stopped and wondered whether he could keep doing this. It took him about a year before he could think about making new work. And now he suffered from the anxiety that the gallery in London would do the same thing.

Around him, his studio looked temporary, furnished only with what was necessary. He had taken over the lease from a Canadian painter who had moved back to Montreal shortly after Andrew arrived in Berlin. There were only a few personal items in this space: an old aluminium lamp he'd bought second-hand at a market and now used as a reading lamp. And there was the old Rolleiflex his father had given him for his tenth birthday: the first camera he had ever owned. It sat on a shelf, the lens cap lost, its eye permanently open. He took that camera with him wherever he went, although it was old, scratched and dented and no longer of any real use to him, not for the type of photographs he took now. It took the world and flattened it; in its lens the world lost its depth. But the Rolleiflex was his one tangible record of his father. And it reminded him of the things in life he wanted to hold on to, of the camera's ability to take the world, collect its images and store them securely in its black and airless cavity.

In his studio that morning he could do no work. He was too distracted by his thoughts about Kirsten. Even after they'd stopped living together, their relationship had continued, on and off, for almost ten years. In those years he'd told himself that what was happening between them was only sex and that he could end it whenever he wanted. It wasn't until he'd left for Berlin that he really understood her power over him. She was a woman who, as long as he had known her, had had a flicker of panic in her eyes, the look of a person who fears they are drowning. He wanted to understand what had happened to her and, sitting there in his studio, he realised that he would have to return to Sydney in order to do so. In fact, it occurred to him, the timing was ideal. His mother had been dropping hints recently about wanting to see him again. He could visit his mother and find out what had happened to Kirsten without having to involve Dom in the whole messy business of why he'd left Sydney. He could be back in Berlin by the time Dom returned from Cologne.

•

He left that afternoon, packing his suitcase with all his clean clothes and his camera, just in case he saw something in Sydney that appealed to him.

At the airport, while he was waiting at the gate for his flight to be called, he called Dom's mobile. It was late in the afternoon and the light was becoming thin and metallic. She would have arrived in Cologne by now. But the call went straight through to her voicemail. He opened his mouth to speak then closed it again and ended the call. He wondered how Dom would react when, later, she heard this empty message on her phone. He imagined her pressing the phone to her ear and hearing nothing but static, like the sound inside a shell.

3

In the aeroplane, he had no awareness of movement. With the window shades down and the lights dimmed, the plane felt still, as though suspended from a cord in mid-air, like a mobile over a child's bed. Time was distorted around him. He slept deeply most of the way to Sydney and woke before they landed to find his breakfast laid out on the tray in front of him, sealed in plastic and foil.

He had used his frequent flyer points to buy the flight, which meant a four-hour stopover in Bangkok between connecting flights, during which he'd managed a snatched conversation with Dom. He'd told her the reason for his trip and that he'd be back in Berlin the day after her. She had wanted to know why it was so important for him to find out about this woman.

But he wasn't sure he could explain it yet, even to himself.

'I love you,' he said.

'*Ich dich auch*,' she replied.

•

When the plane landed in Sydney, he shuffled along behind the other passengers. He moved awkwardly through the customs hall, teetering forward as he took the escalator down to the baggage carousels. After so long on board the plane, sleeping and flying against time, it took him a while to become aware of his own edges again.

After being out of the country for so long, hearing the Australian accent again made him bristle, the way the voices floated, uninvited, into his head. Two women behind him were discussing whether or not to go back and buy another bottle of duty-free vodka and the man beside him was asking the customs officer whether he should declare the chocolate he'd brought back with him from Switzerland. People became an amplified version of themselves when they travelled, their good and bad qualities turned up a few notches.

He queued for a taxi. When he got into the car, talkback radio blared from the front, the honeyed tones of a voice that seemed to be coaxing the world into outrage.

'Leichhardt, please,' he said as the car bumped over the speed hump and turned a corner to drive out of the airport.

Along the expressway, the nature strips divided the lanes of traffic in two. Gymea lilies, their flowers already black, sat like ravaged nests on stilts and the kangaroo paws had turned a dirty orange from exhaust fumes. Houses backed directly onto the road and through breaks in fences he caught glimpses of yards and swimming pools, small and private views of other people's lives.

As they drove towards the city in the late summer light, everything around him looked unreal. The light was brighter than it was in Europe, sharper and somehow crueller. He hadn't prepared himself for it.

•

Along his mother's fence purple hydrangeas bloomed, their round heads like old women's swimming caps. The first sound he heard after he knocked on the door was the squelch of her rubber-soled shoes on the wooden floor. As long as he could remember, his mother had worn flat shoes, like most nurses.

'Andy,' she said as she opened the door, and she walked straight into him, wrapping her arms around him. She was the only person who continued to call him by that name. He wasn't sure, exactly, when people had stopped calling him that and started, instead, to call him Andrew. It had happened gradually, the further away he travelled from childhood, as though the innocence that went with the nickname had thinned and faded and was now finally lost. He rested a cheek on her head. She still used the same shampoo.

After a moment she let go, took a step back and held his shoulders. He saw that a patch of hair near her temple had turned completely white, although the rest of her hair had remained dark, like his.

'What happened?' she asked. 'Why are you home all of a sudden?'

His mother went through her life assuming the worst. And he knew why. She worried that he would die young, as his father had; her greatest fear was outliving him.

He'd only had time to send her a quick email before he left Berlin. *Don't worry about collecting me from the airport*, he'd written, though he knew she wouldn't. She hardly drove anywhere, anymore. She hadn't been into the city in years, though it was barely six kilometres away. Sometimes he wondered why she stayed in Leichhardt. If she wanted to live quietly, why she didn't move to some small coastal town, or to the mountains where her sister lived? But part of him knew exactly why she stayed. Living in the same house for so many years had always been about holding on to the memories of his father.

•

Andrew was eleven when his father died. That day, he came home from school to a silent and empty house for the first time he could remember. All he could hear as he opened the door and walked carefully down the hall were echoes of his own movements. Even before he learnt of his father's death, he knew from the silence that something had been irreversibly lost.

His mother had never told him how his father died; the knowledge remained inside her sunk deep like a stone in a well. As a child he kept thinking that one day, when she stopped feeling sad, she would sit him down and explain everything. But a year had passed and then another year. And he hadn't been told a thing about it. Nor had he dared to ask. From overheard telephone conversations, he had gleaned two facts: 'collapsed' and 'the garden'. Those words were all he ever knew about his father's death.

His mind, though, had filled in the blanks. The absences in his knowledge were transformed into pictures, a sequence of images that ran together in his head. He replayed those scenes so often they had become as real to him as if he'd actually witnessed them. His father stood in their backyard, surveying his vegetable garden. Then, abruptly, he toppled, like Marlon Brando in *The Godfather.*

•

His mother made him a pot of tea in the same striped teapot she'd always used, though the pattern grew more faded each time he sat down to drink from it. He'd once brought her back a new teapot from Delft, hand-painted blue and white, the porcelain so fine it felt soft in his hands. His mother used the things she owned until they had served their purpose. This was what losing someone you loved did to a person: it made it difficult to let go of other things. She would be serving tea from that teapot until the day it broke apart in her hands.

'How's Dom?' she said, sliding onto the stool beside his. His mother's movements had become smaller and more horizontal as she'd aged.

'She's fine, Mum,' he said, not quite meeting her gaze. 'I had to see to a few things back here before my exhibition next month. It has nothing to do with Dom and me.'

'So everything's okay then?' Her tone was tentative, as if she was aware she was asking for too much. His mother had never met Dom and he tried to keep their relationship to himself. He wanted to hold on to this new privacy he'd acquired from living abroad. His mother had lost her husband at a young age and seemed deter-mined, since then, to know everything she could about Andrew, as though knowing the details might prevent another loss. He couldn't bring himself to speak to her about Kirsten straight away. He'd always felt he could not mention death to his mother without reminding her of the death they both lived by.

'When's your opening?'

'Mid-March. I have to send the galleries all the images by the end of the month.'

'That soon?'

He nodded and they both looked at the calendar on the wall. It was the third of February; he'd lost a day in transit.

She sighed heavily. 'How long are you staying?'

'I'm flying back next Saturday. Is that okay with you?'

'That soon? Of course,' she said.

They spoke easily about other things: his mother's sister, the walk-in wardrobes she'd recently had installed. He told her that the tenants in his apartment in Darlinghurst were moving out in two weeks and the agent would be advertising for new ones. Though he couldn't always be open with his mother, he felt at least that around her, he never had to pretend; he didn't have to project the air of confidence that the rest of the world expected of him. He felt the same way around Dom.

4

He arranged to meet Stewart the following afternoon at the Nag's Head in Glebe, the pub they used to drink at when they were students. If he had someone he could call a best friend, a friend who had travelled with him for life, Stewart was it, though they saw each other rarely now. When they were still at school, Stewart had lived on the other side of Parramatta Road in Petersham and for many years they had spent the afternoons together, until Andrew discovered photography and it changed the way he related to the people around him. He always made a point of seeing Stewart when he was back in Sydney, even when he had very little time. Their lives had run at parallels and seeing Stewart each time he returned had become a way of measuring himself.

He walked in through the front bar, hearing the familiar sound of glasses shuddering together as the barman lifted a tray of schooners onto a stack, and took a seat at a small table near the beer garden. On the wall above the table was a picture of an English hunting scene, men in red coats riding horses with beagles trailing at their heels. Ahead of them, foxes ran with their heads turned back towards their pursuers, gaunt flashes of red, the whites of their eyes holding an awareness of their fate.

Stewart arrived wearing a business shirt with the top button undone; a tie dangled from the left pocket of his pants. Since he'd graduated from university, Stewart looked to be permanently straining; the muscles around his neck were thick, giving him a top-heavy appearance, and he walked with his head down, as though peering over a ledge. Over the years his hair had turned slowly and prematurely grey. Stewart lifted his satchel over his shoulder and they hugged awkwardly, patting each other forcefully on the back.

'I wasn't expecting you to come home so soon,' Stewart said, when he came back to their table with two beers.

'How was the wedding?' he asked without meeting Stewart's gaze. Stewart had been married six months ago and Andrew had not flown back for the wedding. Instead he'd sent an email apologising. *Break a leg*, he'd written, as though the whole thing were a performance for Stewart's family and friends.

'Oh, great, man. It was just a big party. You know, an *expensive* party,' Stewart said, and laughed. 'It would have been great if you could have made it.'

Andrew had explained at the time that he was too busy preparing for his upcoming exhibition, but the truth was he didn't want to risk bumping into Kirsten, not after he'd left Sydney without any explanation. He couldn't bear facing the accusation in her eyes.

'And how's . . . your wife?' He couldn't believe it; as the sentence left his mouth, he couldn't recall her name, although he'd known her since they were in their twenties.

There was a part of him, some pocket deep inside, that envied people like Stewart—people who had fallen in love young and who'd given up other things in their lives in order to remain that way.

'Louise is great. You know, we've been together forever, so nothing really changed for us, but we did buy a house in Stanmore.'

This was what happened to people like Stewart and Louise: their lives followed a certain pattern and it never deviated from the path other people expected them to take. There was a feeling that often took hold of him when Stewart and he were together now, that their lives had veered too far apart and what they were doing with these dinners and drinks was trying to restore something they'd already lost.

'Good for you. Property is expensive here. It's much

cheaper in Berlin. I'm thinking of selling my apartment in Darlinghurst so we can buy something there.'

'Really?' Stewart's eyes were alight at the mention of Berlin. 'I loved Berlin, when we visited. You don't find the language a barrier?'

'Oh no, not really. I know enough to get by.' He knew the names of things, but he had never learnt how to fit those words together into sentences and the truth was that being around Dom made him lazy about learning. When he was alone, he moved through the city, pointing to what he wanted in shops and speaking in nouns and he didn't mind not understanding the things being said around him. It afforded him a quietness in which he could be alone with his thoughts.

'Do you think you'd ever come back here to live?' Stewart asked, his voice scooting higher suddenly, wanting some sort of reassurance from him.

'I don't know. There are a lot more opportunities for me to exhibit over there. Europe is a much bigger market. Also my work sells better there.' He watched the disappointment trickle through Stewart's expression.

'Well, I guess it would be difficult with Dom, wouldn't it?'

He nodded an agreement and stroked the sweating glass with his finger.

Stewart looked down and then back up again and there was a looseness to his expression, the face of a person who has information they are not quite sure how to share.

'Have you heard any more about Kirsten since you came back?' Stewart said softly, looking into his beer. There was a single line of bubbles floating to the surface.

'No, I haven't heard anything,' he said. Weary now, in the fug of his jet lag, he was no longer sure that he actually wanted to hear more. He felt himself recoiling in anticipation of the details.

Stewart leant forward, bent over his beer, as though the words he spoke were very heavy and had dragged him there. 'They've stopped the search. For the body. I heard after I sent the email to you.' He looked to be on the verge of tears. 'Louise found out from Kirsten's mother that there'll be a service for her. Tomorrow, actually.'

'The body?'

Stewart nodded. 'Your mum didn't hear anything about it? It was reported on the news a few weeks back, as a suspected drowning in Lake George.'

'Drowning?' he said distantly. 'My mum doesn't watch much television anymore.' And he hadn't told her, reverting to the familiar instinct he'd always had to protect his mother from the things that might upset her. 'Kirsten drowned?' He could hardly fit his mouth around the word.

Stewart nodded sadly. 'They think so. Louise is going to the service. And I will if I can. It's just there's something on at work. I'm not sure if I can get out of it.' He gestured vaguely, as if trying to offer Andrew more of an explanation with the movement of his hands.

'Had you seen her recently? Did Louise and Kirsten keep in touch?' He'd always wondered if Stewart knew what went on between Andrew and Kirsten for all those years after they'd officially broken up. He'd never spoken about it—mostly he felt embarrassed by it.

Stewart licked his lips. 'Louise tried, I think. She always made the effort. We invited her to our wedding. She RSVP'd but never showed up. I think Louise had plans for dinner with her a few months ago, but Kirsten pulled out on the day. Louise feels bad that she didn't try harder, but I don't know; you can't force someone to see you.'

Andrew stood to go to the toilet and a space seemed to have opened at his feet, like a rupture in the earth's crust. Around him, this old place was the same as it had always been, but his world had now changed. A part of it that had once meant something to him, a slice of his own personal history, was missing.

•

When he thought about Kirsten, what he thought of most were her silences. She was a woman who was always on the verge of speaking, of looking away then back towards him with the sense that there was something important she had to say. Her silences were intoxicating; they held the promise that one day he might know what they were hiding. But she had always kept her secrets to herself.

He continued to think about her in the years since he moved to Berlin. Sometimes he went through phases where he thought about her every day. He had loved her, but it was the sort of love that was like falling. It was young love, the love you can only ever have when you are still finding yourself. At the time he sometimes thought, *This is it*. He'd tried to make himself believe those words, but the sensation lasted only a short time. He'd loved her as best he could in that clumsy, incomplete way people do when they are too young to surrender themselves to another person. But she needed more from him than he was able to give. He wanted her, but he didn't want her problems.

They separated and lived apart. But he still saw her, sometimes regularly and other times not for months. Occasionally he thought he still loved her, but there was something very intense about Kirsten, and her need for him. He was never exactly sure what it was about her that kept reeling him back in.

•

Later, when he came home from the pub, the house was still and his mother was already asleep. As a shift worker, she had always taken her sleep when she could and he had learnt to be quiet and alone from a young age. He turned on his laptop and sat it on his lap, the spool of the hard drive whirring against his knees. He searched for news articles about Kirsten, hoping for definite answers, but her disappearance was described in ambiguous and inconclusive terms. There were photos of Lake George, its surface mirrored, like a puddle of mercury that had settled on grass. The silvery stretch of water reflected the world the wrong way up. The abandoned car left beside the lake, cordoned off by yellow tape. All these articles about her—was this what she wanted, for the world to pay attention to her? Maybe, after years of silence, this had been her final scream.

There was an interview with a man who had been picnicking by the lake with his family and had seen Kirsten sitting in the car. He had glimpsed her walking out through the vaporous haze towards the lake. At the time of the interview, they were still searching for the body. He read article after article, but none of them told a coherent story.

He turned off the computer and as it slowed and wheezed itself to sleep, he thought about what it would be like to disappear. To leave the past behind, to walk away from it and all the ways in which it tarnished you and held you back. All you would have then was a future. He had felt this way when he left for Berlin: that he was stepping into his future and, as he did so, the door to his past would close permanently behind him.

•

That night he spoke to Dom.

'How are the kids? Are you sick of them yet?'

'Of course I'm not. They're wonderful. They try so hard, but I worry some of them try *too* hard. They want to grow up to be dancers, every one of them. And all I want to do is to tell them how difficult it is, about the injuries and the hours and hours of practice, but of course I can't spoil their dreams. That would be too cruel. I have to let them learn for themselves.'

Dom always felt this sadness for the children she taught, as though she saw in them the girl she had once been, young and supple and too full of optimism.

'How is your mother?' she asked, and he could tell that she was lying on her back because her voice was caught in her throat.

'Good, I think. She's glad to see me,' he said. 'But I haven't actually told her about Kirsten yet.'

'You haven't told her?'

'I guess I just don't want to upset her. My mother can be a bit sensitive sometimes.'

Dom laughed. 'God, she probably thinks we're fighting or something.' She paused. 'Say hello to her from me.'

He said he would, although Dom and his mother had never met. He hadn't told Dom the whole truth about Kirsten either; for him it was somehow easier to be silent.

5

For a time they had been happy together, he, Kirsten, Louise and Stewart, their lives wound closely together. They studied at the same university, went out together and created a comfortable existence structured around their small group. And he could see the future, their lives ahead of them as they grew old together: the dinners, the gatherings, the careers and families, stitching themselves into each other's lives. It had given him a sort of comfort at a time of uncertainty.

He met Kirsten at a barbecue at Stewart's house on a bright Saturday that made everything appear new. Kirsten was a friend of Louise, and what he first noticed about her was her smile. It was large and generous, so broad it seemed to be compensating for something. She was quick and stealthy, turning up at his elbow with a tray of meatballs in one hand and a jar of toothpicks in the other. Her skin was white, and her hair a black so complete that it absorbed the sun's light with a gleam.

She spoke in runs of words, lodging them into the conversation between other people's and looking upwards as though she was retrieving the words from somewhere over his head. Her voice had a lightness to it; it was so soft he sometimes missed the words. Even then he had a sense—from her eagerness to please, to be liked by other people—that she was hiding some sort of emptiness inside her, a small black void. He knew something about that feeling himself and he realised that they were drawn together because of what they both lacked.

Like Andrew, Kirsten was studying fine arts, majoring in drawing. It seemed like such a modest ambition. He asked her what she drew and she said she liked to draw faces best. The first time he saw one of her drawings he was mesmerised by the number of tiny strokes, as though the world she imagined was constructed from small lines.

They met for coffee and she drew a picture for him in pencil: a copy of an Alfred Stieglitz photograph of Georgia O'Keeffe with her hands held up before her. He knew that photograph well; he had studied at length the way shadow fell under the strong line of her jaw.

When he saw that drawing, he knew Kirsten had something rare: a feeling for light. Her shadings on the page mimicked the way light fell. She had produced this just with her hands. He reached across the table and he pressed his lips to her fingertips, and then to her mouth.

They fell inwards together. For almost three years, their existence was a happy, domestic routine; they were creating a new life for themselves, the buoyant existence of two people in love. It was Kirsten who suggested they move in together. He'd always suspected that her childhood had been troubled, although she never spoke of it and he never invited her to. There was a stiffness about her when she mentioned her family; her body became tense, fighting something inside her, perhaps an urge to let everything out.

She was always in such a hurry to move their relationship along, to fortify their intimacy and make what they had into something permanent, wanting to bind them together at an age when nothing was fixed. She rushed to bring them together, to have them live in the same apartment, to commit to him, in the way of someone in a hurry to leave something behind. He didn't know, then, that there is a danger to going about life too fast.

He left his mother's home and moved in with Kirsten. It was only on leaving that he understood the sadness that had clung to his mother's existence. He had lived with it for so long that he had stopped noticing how it affected him, this sadness they both had, a thin white membrane around them, sticky and wet as a caul. Whenever he went back home to visit her, he experienced a sudden claustrophobia. The unspoken grief surrounding his father's death had taken something from him. As he grew older he realised that the effortless way most people spoke about their own lives was more difficult for him.

●

The love Kirsten and he made in that time together was unlike anything he had experienced before. They seemed to be searching each other's bodies for something, as though they wanted to push each other's flesh apart and crawl inside. They wanted to get beneath the surface of their skin, to forget their own troubling thoughts. It became something dark and suffocating, an obsession, and for a while nothing else in his life held the power over him that Kirsten had in bed.

There was a window in the apartment they shared, facing onto the street, where the streetlight thrummed its orange light into the darkness. They couldn't afford curtains for their windows and the room was permanently illuminated, even at night. He still remembered one morning when they woke, the length of their bodies pressed together, and he rolled over and kissed her breast. The skin on her nipples was fragile and whenever he touched it, he had the feeling that it could be easily torn. She rose from the bed and walked to the window, naked. She stood there, as if she wanted the world to see her, to disclose herself physically, in a way she was unable to in words. She wanted to reveal and she wanted to remain unseen. She wanted the world to know her, but the greater urge was the one that caused her to withhold. And it had stayed with her, it seemed, until her death.

They made love by that window more times than he could count, him behind her as she looked out, and there was something erotic about being inside her and yet unable to see the expression on her face. She would stand and walk to the window, beckoning him to follow. Kirsten could always pick her moments; just when he found himself wondering, when he looked at her and felt a cool flicker of disdain and the early shine of their relationship had worn away, she would walk to the window and reel him in.

He had asked other women to stand the same way, beside a window, naked, in an effort to re-create the feeling it had evoked when she was exposed but still his, the slippery sensation of ownership and control. But it never worked. He had looked at those other women, trying to feel something, but whatever he felt, it was always something less than desire. He had even tried it with Dom once, at the start of their relationship, when they were in his apartment with the window that faced onto the park.

'Move over to the window,' he'd said that day, when she slipped from bed naked one morning, ready to stretch.

'To the window?' she said. Her face was still marked with the creases of her pillow.

He nodded.

'I'm naked and it's cold,' she said, gesturing at her body and laughing lightly at him. And with those words, she broke the spell. His relationship with Dom became something new; from that moment onwards he had stopped looking behind him for love.

•

There was a particular day that seemed to contain the moment when he understood that things between he and Kirsten could not last. He was in his Honours year. It was a hot day; the dense sort of heat that causes discomfort. He'd come home to their apartment one afternoon after a photo shoot for his final project.

He was photographing a still life, an image of a delicate porcelain teacup that he had broken along one side and glued together again with araldite. It was a Wedgwood teacup he'd bought new at David Jones for far more money than he could afford at the time and he had made the break carefully with a chisel and vice in the sculpture room at his college. He was pleased with how neatly it had broken in two; there had always been the danger that it would shatter or that the break would not be clean.

He'd been working on the photograph for days, arranging the lights so they caught the fine break in the porcelain, using wire and tape to lever the light in different directions. He'd photographed the cup hundreds of times, until he had the feeling that he wasn't preserving it on film but was somehow destroying it. Eventually, he captured the image he wanted, so that the crack in the china was just visible, but the cup still looked delicate and whole. He called that picture 'Porcelain'. Some people would look at that photo and see a beautiful piece of china and others would see only that it was flawed. He was speaking to two audiences and every piece of art he had produced since spoke this way, with a forked tongue. These were the small ruptures that, over the years, came to characterise his work.

Since college, he had devoted himself to photographing faces. He had become known for photographing people who were damaged in some way. If ever anyone asked him why, he would say that he wanted to take photographs that showed people's thoughts rather than how they looked. His photographs helped him see inside other people.

Kirsten, meanwhile, had deferred her studies for a year and took a job in an office in the city. She seemed to derive a sort of pleasure from the routine of waking up early each morning and preparing herself for the working day. He watched her sometimes, from bed, the way she eased herself into her skirt and slipped her legs into stockings. She had the look about her of performance, as if she was an actor playing a role and she had left her real self behind in the wings. She had said that she needed a year off to think things over. She wasn't sure she was studying the right subject and she needed some time to make a decision, although she was already two years into her degree. It was almost as though she was afraid of reaching the end, because it would mean she would have to confront what came next; she would have to take her art out into the world and allow it to be judged.

Kirsten arrived home not long after he'd walked in. He was in the kitchen, drinking a glass of water. Outside, the clouds were dense in the sky, a dusty grey, the air still; a storm was about to break. He thought he heard a rumble from outside, but one so distant it might have been a passing truck. She sat down on the couch.

'I'm not feeling well,' she said, leaning back on the lounge, holding the back of her hand to her forehead.

That was another thing about Kirsten: there was always something wrong with her. She never complained very strenuously and her words were always gentle, but almost always she had to tell him that in some small way she was ill. Sometimes it was her throat. At other times she had pains in her back. Once she even told him she thought the pain in her stomach might be an ulcer, that her father had once had a stomach ulcer and maybe she was getting one now too. Eventually, he learnt to ignore her; it wasn't that he didn't care, but that he never knew what he could do or say to help.

'Oh yeah?' He washed out the glass he'd been drinking from and started to dry it. The glass made a small squeak of protest against the moist tea towel.

'I've got a sore throat. Do I feel hot to you?'

'It's a hot day,' he said, still twisting the cloth inside the glass.

'Yeah, but hot like I've got a temperature.'

He put the glass in the cupboard and opened the fridge. 'What do you feel like for dinner?'

'Why do you always do that?' She stood and walked towards him. 'Whenever I'm feeling sick you just completely ignore me. It's really inconsiderate.'

He didn't respond.

'Don't you care if I'm ill?'

'Of course I do,' he said. 'I just—' A hot feeling crept up his windpipe.

'What?' She took his hand and held the back of it to her forehead. He could feel the warmth of her skin. He pulled his hand away.

'It's just—' he started to say again. But what could he say? How could he tell her that all these things that were wrong with her, what she needed from him, overwhelmed him?

He went to their bedroom. Kirsten's clothes were strewn across the bedroom floor. One shoe stuck out from underneath the bed, the bedclothes were crumpled and the room smelt of body odour. He opened the windows, flicking the locks and pushing them up so quickly they screamed as they slid. He started picking up clothes and throwing them into the dirty-clothes basket, surprised at how angry he was suddenly. And what he realised as he walked through their room, picking up stray items of clothing, was that what he really wanted, more than to be with her, was to be alone.

He didn't break up with her straight away; he didn't have the courage. Instead he became quieter, withdrawing into himself until what they had was no longer a relationship but two people who had the appearance of one, eating meals at the same table and sharing a bed, lying quietly together each night as though there were tombstones at their heads rather than pillows. Kirsten recognised what was happening before he said a word.

On the day they split up, he came home late. Kirsten was in the kitchen and he stopped in the middle of the lounge room, standing there with his bag over one shoulder. She was still made up from work, with fissures in her lipstick and a residue of red. He hardly needed to say anything at all. It was the week after his final-year show had opened and a gallery had contacted him to express an interest in representing him. He had an interview the following week and he'd spent the day assembling his portfolio with a mounting sense of excitement. From then on, he thought, his life would follow the clear and silver line of success, and everything that might hold him back from what he wanted would have to be cast aside. (As it happened, the gallery never called him back after his interview and it took him five more years to find representation. By then he was almost thirty and his youth lay behind him.)

He could remember very few of the words he actually used, though he would recall saying, *I just can't keep doing this every day.* The truth was, he wanted to help her but couldn't. And he had to focus on photography; he didn't feel he had a choice about it—everything else in his life was secondary. When he told Kirsten he was moving out, she stood in the kitchen with her red mouth open, gaping like a wound.

Stewart texted him the details of the memorial service early that morning. It was being held at a church in Lavender Bay, on the other side of the harbour. He knew Kirsten's mother was religious, but in their time together Kirsten and he had never been into a church and he'd never heard her speak of God.

He arrived at the church in a taxi, late, after the service had already begun. The church was dark inside and he stood in the aisle for a moment waiting for his eyes to adjust to the lack of light. He took a seat on the last pew, with several vacant rows in front of him. All he saw from where he sat were the backs of heads he didn't recognise, all cast down. At the front of the church the minister read from a Bible. He spoke in waves of words, spoken hundreds of times before, about people who were now buried in the earth. They were words that knew nothing of Kirsten, about the way she lived. Behind him, the stained-glass windows glowed in green, yellow and red.

He scanned the bodies in front of him looking for Stewart's wife, Louise. Kirsten's mother and stepfather were there too, presumably, though he wasn't sure he'd recognise them; he'd only met them once. What would he say to them now? That he was sorry for their loss? But they had been losing Kirsten for years, since he'd known her and probably before then. He hadn't really come here to express his condolences; he had come here to understand what had happened to her. To pick it apart and trace it back, step by step, to find out exactly where things had gone wrong.

At the front of the church was a casket made from polished blond wood. The lilies on top were sullen and dark. The coffin must have been empty, since no body had been found. He wondered what would happen at the end of the service, whether they would pick up this weightless box and carry it down the aisle, going through those motions, pretending that this death was just like any other, though there were no bones to grieve over.

With a sudden spasm of memory, Andrew thought of his father's funeral. This was the first funeral he'd been to since; he'd always made excuses, he'd even told lies in order to avoid them. At his father's funeral, he'd been a pallbearer and he'd helped carry the coffin from the church. He remembered feeling the gaze of the whole church on him, a congregation of pale faces, as he walked unsteadily down the aisle, and feeling as though he had to smile, that he was expected to look like he was coping, and that by gritting his teeth and wishing for all this attention to be behind him he was letting his father down.

The only other coherent memory he had of that day was later, as his father's coffin was lowered into the ground. He thought how shiny the casket was, that it was such new wood, and how strange it was that it would now be buried in dirt. He'd wondered whether it would stay that way, with the wood gleaming like a freshly varnished violin. He couldn't even locate his mother in that memory, although she must have been there too, stern, steely, fending off grief with crossed arms.

He hadn't thought about his father's death in years, though for a long time it was all he could think of, at school and when he was with his friends. He was constantly distracted by his thoughts, though nobody else seemed to notice this. He became the boy who had lost his father; his father's death had defined him. It was a strange thing, to be defined by a loss. He remembered looking at himself in his school photographs and thinking how different he looked to his peers, that there was an awareness about him that had not yet impressed itself on any of the other children.

Sitting at the back of the church now, he sneezed without warning. Once, twice, three times in succession. It must have been the dust in the hall. A few people turned around and looked at him with dark eyes. He sat completely still, but there was a tickle in his nose and he worried it might happen again. The rest of the room stood to sing a hymn and he tripped over the footrest in his hurry to exit the church. He pinched his nose with his fingers to suppress another sneeze. The church organ sounded distant and mournful. Outside the sunlight was brash; the heavy light and thick warm air made movement difficult.

He sat down on a seat in the park nearby and stayed there for a moment with his head between his knees. When he sat upright, he loosened his tie. He turned and saw, behind him, the church starting to empty, bodies spilling out onto the grass. He tried to identify Kirsten's parents among the people clad in funereal tones, blacks, charcoals and greys. In the sunlight those colours gave the mourners a definite outline. Their movements were slow with grief. There was a woman standing next to the minister and taking people's hands in her own. He thought this might have been Kirsten's mother, but from this distance he couldn't be sure. From where he stood she looked to be swaying on her feet, perhaps swooning with sadness.

He looked at the other people. Stewart's wife Louise would be among them, but she was the only person he would know. If he walked over he would stand there awkwardly, trying to find someone to talk to him. A shadow fell on him. He'd had this experience often; it seemed to follow him wherever he settled, him standing apart from a larger group, unable to join in.

He decided he would wait until the crowd dispersed and then he would approach the figure he thought could be Kirsten's mother. He would explain who he was and that they had met before. Perhaps she would remember and be glad to see him there.

He turned away from the mourners. Between the buildings, he could see a thin sliver of the harbour and he sat and watched the windswept blue. That was something he missed when he was in Berlin: he never saw the sea. Sometimes he longed for the definite blue of the ocean, something that helped him to understand where he was in relation to other things.

A hearse drove by in front of him and when he turned back to the church, the crowd had dispersed; they were unlocking the doors of their cars and following Kirsten's empty coffin down the road towards the place where she would be laid to rest. It was too late now to speak to her mother.

He found himself hoping that Kirsten would be buried near water. He stood and watched the procession drive down the road and away from him.

•

He went home and called Dom in a daze of emotion. He told her about the funeral service, how they hadn't found the body but there'd been a coffin anyway.

'Was this woman special to you?' Dom asked gently.

'I suppose,' he said evasively. 'But I hadn't spoken to her since I came to Berlin.'

Dom had spoken of old lovers, but he'd never been able to share his past with her. There had really only been Kirsten and he wasn't even sure what to make of that relationship himself; it was too complicated to reduce to words. He'd left Sydney to escape it: the strange combination of love and aversion he felt for her.

For Dom, there had been someone called Dirk.

'Six years,' she had said to him in the dark of her bedroom soon after they met. 'Six years, four years ago.' She spoke his name and he heard, caught up with it, a knot of feeling that was hidden to him, some old pain. He could tell from the way she spoke that it had once engulfed her.

Part of him wanted to tell Dom about Kirsten now, how his relationship with her had coloured everything that came after. That he had allowed it to continue for too long; that he hadn't been able to bring himself to end it cleanly. He wanted to tell Dom because her love was the only thing that could wash away this terrible feeling that what had happened to Kirsten might somehow be his fault.

7

Andrew woke early the next morning. It was just before six and the light outside his window was sheer. He dressed in jeans and a t-shirt and walked out to the lounge room. On the kitchen bench nearby, petals slipped suddenly from the roses in the vase. Through the window, the shadows were narrow and long in the backyard, stretched geometric shapes that might have been cast by tall buildings.

He loved this time of the day in Sydney, when the city was still quiet, hushed; he could almost pretend in those moments that he had it to himself. Later, when it awoke and the noise rose to a clamour, he was aware that he would have to compete for space and quiet with the city's other inhabitants.

On his mother's wall still hung his final year work, *Porcelain*. Over the years, he'd given her other prints of his more successful work, but this was the only photograph she'd hung in the house. He remained aware that photography was what formed the bridge between his old life and his new one. It connected what he had been to what he had become.

When he took photography as a subject at high school, cameras weren't yet digital and he preferred it that way. He still used film. He loved the smell of it, that it was something which could be touched rather than an amount of data measured in bytes. Digital photography had made things easier and less messy, it had made the whole process quicker and more efficient, but he couldn't help feeling that some of the mystery had been lost.

At high school, the darkroom was his domain. His teacher had given him the key and nobody but Andrew went in there outside class. It was downstairs in the basement and he had always liked descending those stairs, knowing that he was entering a space in which the rules were known to him. They only ever printed in black and white at school, but he had enjoyed the limitation of it; he liked the way it took everything that was bright and alive and reduced it to something less.

He loved the warm chemical baths that he submerged his photos in, too; they smelt personal to him, like bodily fluids. There was always the moment of anticipation when the pictures started to emerge evenly, poured across the paper. He sometimes wished he could prolong that moment, the instant before the image was set, before he knew whether what had been recorded on paper had lived up to the idea he had had for it.

Afterwards, he hung the photos up with pegs, like socks on a clothesline. He sometimes wished that his life had remained that simple, that he could spend hours alone in the darkroom and emerge blinking into the sunlight, more sure of himself and better able to face the world. He'd become a photographer in his last years of high school and those years had shaped him, formed his identity; laid down inside him like sedimentary rocks.

Later, he went to art school and focused on learning his craft, becoming lean and serious about photography. Like an athlete, he became efficient at just that one thing; it had become the only thing he could do well.

He hovered in the kitchen and opened the fridge; he was hungry, but reluctant to eat his mother's food. He walked down the back steps outside into the yard and the cold air prickled his skin. He usually avoided coming out here. This was where his father had died and, from the age of eleven until he left home, he spent most of his time indoors. He wasn't superstitious. He didn't believe in ghosts. He'd had to contemplate death from a young age and he knew that there was nothing after death; that, with it, a person slipped beneath the surface of a vast black sea and they were gone.

It wasn't his father's ghost that had done the haunting, but his own memories of him. When he was younger he'd wished that, since his father was gone, his memories of his father would leave him too. At that age it seemed unfair, even cruel, that his father could be dead, but the memories remained as though his father still lived. He wanted to push the memories aside, to expel them, to sink them into the same unreachable place where his father now lay. And on a day-to-day level, he felt this was possible, that he could manage to forget him, that the man who had been his father became an outline— until the whole man returned to him suddenly, in an irresistible flood of feeling.

The vegetable patch took up almost half the yard and the plants had grown larger than he remembered: a knotted mass, tangles of tomatoes and a pumpkin vine that crept across the yard towards the garden shed in search of new territory. He pushed his way between the rows, the wet leaves brushing his legs as he passed. Hidden between the leaves of one plant was the curved shape of an eggplant, its skin secretive and dark. Along the back fence the old passionfruit clung to the palings, green fruit tugged at the vine and the flowers were delicate tendrils of white and purple, concentric circles, like pretty eyes that shifted in the breeze.

'Andrew?'

He heard his mother's voice behind him. He turned suddenly with the same sick feeling he'd had as a boy, when he thought he had upset her in some way. Just by being out there, he felt, he was reminding her of his father's absence.

'I'm making breakfast for us,' she said from the back veranda, standing in her dressing-gown. Dressed that way she looked small and frail, depleted by age. He walked up to the back steps, went inside and stood on the other side of the kitchen bench as his mother finished preparing their breakfast. The kitchen cupboards were painted a shiny lime green and the drawers were wooden and prone to jam halfway, having to be eased in and out with a wriggle.

'Oh, I forgot—this came for you,' his mother said, pushing an envelope addressed to him across the bench. Normally, she sent anything that came in the post for him over to Berlin, which meant he usually received his mail late. He picked it up—the envelope was clean and white and bore all the markings of a bill. But when he opened it, it was a letter from the Museum of Contemporary Art in Sydney advising that two of his photographs would be included in an exhibition of contemporary photographs that was opening the following month. An invitation to the opening was enclosed, on which his name was printed in embossed gold letters.

The museum had acquired two of his photographs several years before, but there had been no interest in his work from them since. By next month, he would be back in Berlin with Dom. He wondered if he should suggest to his mother that she go in his place, but he knew she wouldn't.

The electric stove in the kitchen was old; the hot element glowed in a coil of red. Steam from the saucepan had misted the kitchen windows. His mother turned the stove off and lifted the pan into the kitchen sink. She'd made hard-boiled eggs and toast, the meal she'd often made for breakfast when he was a boy; it was a nurse's meal, quick, easy and nourishing.

They ate together at the bench, then she readied herself for work. He still remembered the morning of his mother's first day back at work after his father's death. He said goodbye to her through the gauze of the flyscreen door, her fingers still attached to the door handle. It was the only time he'd seen her cry. She was frozen there behind the fine crisscross of wire, her face pixelated by the gauze. Her image was uncertain and blurry, though her sadness was palpable and real. She didn't say a word, but withdrew her fingers from the door and turned to leave. Her small, diminished body disappeared down the front steps and across the front lawn to the gate. In the sky a black cockatoo wailed over her head.

When he removed his hands from the gauze they tasted of salt. It hurt him to see his mother engulfed in sadness and to know there was nothing he could do to help her. It caused a physical pain in his chest. From then on he made an effort never to show his sadness in her presence, never to even think about his father when she was there. He swore he would never cry in front of her and he never did.

He knew photography was somehow connected to this. In photographs there were no feelings, only tangible objects. He accumulated images and eliminated emotions and every photo he'd taken, every success he had with it, was moving him away from this terrible time in his life.

●

That night, he dialled Dom's number and took the phone out to the back veranda so that he wouldn't disturb his mother as she slept.

'Hi. It's me.' He thought of her strong jaw and her dark coiled hair. How it had smelt of lavender on the first night they'd spent together and every night since.

'Hi,' she said. 'How are you?' He could hear her breathing over the phone; she might have been standing at his shoulder, though he knew she was very far away.

'I'm fine. I still feel a bit jet-lagged though. And I don't really know where to start to find more information about Kirsten.'

'You only found out about her death a few days ago and now you are on the other side of the world. It must be disorientating.' Dom had always possessed a clarity he lacked, an ability to understand how another person felt.

'I know. It's also because they didn't find the body. I'm not sure it will really sink in until I find out what happened to her. I haven't really been able to speak to her family about it yet. They didn't say anything about what happened at the funeral.'

There was a pause, then she said, 'I was thinking, would you like me to come over? To Australia, I mean. I'm sure I'll find someone who can cover the rest of my classes here. I've actually never been to Sydney—it might be a good time to finally make the trip.' Her tone was tentative, the words halting. 'And it would be nice to meet your mother.'

He knew immediately he didn't want Dom to come. He wanted her to stay where she was until he could return to her.

'I don't know,' he said.

'You don't know?' she repeated, articulating each word carefully. After almost three years together, this was all he had to offer her. This ambivalence.

He wanted to find out what had happened to Kirsten, that was all. He didn't want the additional complication of having Dom there with him. He wanted to preserve their life as it was in Berlin, so that he could return to it.

Maybe, in truth, he didn't want her to know this part of him, the part that belonged in Sydney. The version of him that had struggled for years without success, who'd treated Kirsten badly. He wanted to quarantine that part of his life from Dom, to protect her from it. In Berlin he could live with everything he'd made with his life; in Sydney he was aware of all the ways in which he'd fallen short.

When he didn't respond, she said, 'Tell me this, do you love me?' The word was soft in her mouth, the 'v' pronounced as an 'f'. *Lofe*, she always said; what she felt for him was *lofe*.

'Come on, Dom, of course I love you. And I'll be home soon—there's no need for you to come all this way. I just want to get this done as quickly as possible then fly home and focus on the London exhibition. We can come out again together another time, when it's less rushed. Maybe later this year?'

As he said the word 'home', he realised that something about the way he viewed the world had shifted. He understood that the place where he stood was no longer where he belonged; his home was the place that he and Dom had created for themselves. And now he had said something that threatened it.

Dom exhaled slowly, audibly, a low heave that sounded as though she was dislodging something from her chest. 'I don't know. You don't want me there. What am I supposed to think? I've never met your mother. Sometimes I feel like I don't really know you at all. Sometimes I think that's the way you prefer it.'

8

On Monday afternoon, he walked around Leichhardt. The streets were so familiar to him that he didn't even have to concentrate on where he was going. He tried not to think about the conversation he'd had with Dom. He hadn't spoken to her the day before at all. Instead, he focused on the fact that they'd both be back in Berlin soon and he could smooth things over between them when they were together. Once he understood what had happened to Kirsten, once he knew how to make sense of things, he could explain it all to Dom.

He lost track of where he was, listening to the internal sounds of his body: his breath; his heartbeat, steady and rhythmic. As he walked, his thoughts scattered away from him like tossed coins. He found himself in front of a school. The buildings were tall, their thick walls made of red bricks. Pictures were taped to the windows, facing outwards, images drawn in crayon by small and imprecise hands. He read the sign LEICHHARDT PUBLIC SCHOOL and had the sensation of moving back into himself. This was his old primary school, but it looked somehow more exposed than his memory of it, too close to the street and the chaos of the city. When he had been there, it had felt secluded.

Mostly, his memories of it were the view from inside, looking out the window during classes and realising, as other students put their heads down to work, that he hadn't been listening to what was said and was unsure what he was supposed to be doing.

The playground was empty now. He glanced at his watch; it was quarter past three. He assumed that school must be over for the day. But even as he had the thought a bell rang and suddenly the school was swarming with green bodies. He stayed there gripping the fence, watching the bodies, small and busy, forming groups and separating, moving like ants.

His eye was caught by a young girl walking slowly through the bodies with her bag slung over one shoulder. Her hat dangled from one finger, bobbing on its elasticised band. The straw hat had buckled on one side.

Her hair was blonde, the colour of barley. When she came closer he thought at first that she was pulling a face because the left side of her mouth was slack. When she smiled at one of her friends, though, he noticed that she smiled with only the right side of her mouth. From where he stood, that part of her face looked melted. She moved around to his side of the fence, eyes on her feet, glancing up from time to time in the direction of Norton Street, as if waiting for someone to arrive. She was only a few metres away from him, and if she hadn't been standing so close, he might have said nothing. He might have walked away and let the idea that had suddenly possessed him pass.

He took a step towards her. 'Hi,' he said.

Growing up, he had no younger siblings or nieces and nephews, and as an adult he'd played no role in the lives of his friends' children. He'd had no experience in talking to children, apart from the models he'd used for photographs, and the young girl seemed to sense his nerves.

'Is your mum or dad coming to pick you up this afternoon?'

Still looking at her feet, she said her mother was coming from work. She spoke so softly he could hardly hear her.

'Okay,' he said. They stood beside each other without speaking and he kept wondering what he should do with his hands.

After a few minutes a woman walked towards them. Her long, dark hair had a silvery sheen in the sun, where it had started to grey. She wore jeans and a tunic that reached her knees. On her feet were flat, practical sandals. She took the girl's head in her hands and kissed her hair. It was a firm gesture that seemed to almost be an expression of relief at having found the young girl still there waiting for her. He wondered where the girl's blonde hair had come from. She held her hat up to her mother, who frowned, and he saw the word *broken* pass over the young girl's lips.

He moved towards them, a sideways movement like a crab's. 'I'm sorry to interrupt you,' he said. He hated scouting for subjects. It was like asking someone he didn't know very well for a favour, even though he paid his models—whether they were professional or not—and most people were glad to be involved. 'I'm a photographer,' he continued. 'I noticed your daughter as I was walking past. I wondered if you would let me take her photograph?'

The woman frowned. 'What sort of a photograph?' she said, moving her arm around her daughter's waist and pulling her closer. The inside of her arm was pale, the two bones in her wrist visible like the underside of a wing. Behind him, the chatter of children peppered his thoughts.

'I'm a photographic artist. You can look me up online. It would be a portrait. I'll pay her. Your daughter has the right look.'

Look. The word repulsed him. It was a word that photographers used, but he didn't like the way it implied that a person's appearance could be slotted into a category.

He hadn't really been thinking about photographs at all until he'd seen her there and an image of her flashed before him against a soft, white background, her hair falling evenly around her face.

Behind the woman he was talking to, he noticed a figure moving towards them. It was a teacher whom he actually recognised, wearing a red shirt and shorts. His socks were pulled up to his knees.

'Can I help you?' the teacher said. A vein in his neck bulged and his face was slightly flushed, the colour of sunburn that hadn't completely faded. Andrew wondered whether it was actually possible that a teacher who'd been there when he was a student was still teaching at the same school. Perhaps he was mistaken. Over the years he had seen so many faces that maybe this man just appeared similar to someone else he knew. But no; Andrew looked at him again and the way he stood, the way he gestured with his hands as he spoke, as though he was demonstrating the dimensions of a box; they were the movements of a person he knew.

'I'm just talking to this girl's mother,' he said. An exhaustion took hold of him. He had too much else to think about and wished he'd said nothing, that he could walk away now and pretend it hadn't happened. 'My name is Andrew Spruce. I'm a photographer. I actually went to school here.' He smiled, trying to muster his charm from somewhere inside him, a place that felt welded shut. He tried to remember the teacher's name.

'You shouldn't be here. These are school premises, not public property. If you don't leave now, I'm afraid I'll have to call the police.'

He couldn't help himself. His reaction against being told what to do was automatic. He pointed out that he wasn't actually on school property, that he'd simply been standing on the footpath.

Something twitched behind the teacher's face; some deep instinct which, after a lifetime of being in control of a classroom, responded badly to being corrected.

'You were talking to this girl without an adult present,' the man said. His voice was low and quavered slightly in response to some suppressed rage. 'There are rules for contacting students. You have to obtain the approval of the principal.'

At that moment, Andrew looked towards the girl's mother and later, when he thought back on the scene, he realised that this was the moment at which she'd decided to give him the benefit of her doubt. There was a softness in her eyes and he understood that she felt sorry for him, was embarrassed by the way he was being berated.

'I'll be reporting this incident to the authorities,' the teacher said, as he left, moving through the clusters of small green bodies remaining in the yard, and the woman moved closer to him, her eyes brown and clear, the colour of weak black tea. 'Do you have a card or something you could give me?' she said, gripping the calico bag that hung over her shoulder and which seemed to be full of books. Behind them the wind rushed through the leaves of a melaleuca tree, the sound, like water over stones.

'I don't have a card with me,' he said. He'd had some business cards made a few years earlier, but they remained sealed in a box somewhere in storage because he was too shy ever to hand them out. 'You can look me up online though; I have a website. I'll write the address down for you. There's an email address for me on the site and I'll give you my mobile number.' He patted his pockets for a pen and the woman found a scrap of paper for him to write on. It was a receipt for some library books; he wrote his contact details on the back.

'Thanks,' she said. 'I'll look you up.' Then she took her daughter's hand and walked down to the pedestrian crossing. There they stopped, the woman looking in both directions cautiously before stepping out, as though very aware of all the things that could go wrong.

He started walking in the opposite direction. He'd only gone about a block from the school when he heard tyres crunch up behind him and the sharp bleep of a siren. He jumped and his heart started to race. A male officer stepped out of the car first.

'We've had a complaint, sir, about a man matching your description who was seen loitering around the school grounds. Was it you?'

He nodded and felt a tight pain across his chest. A female officer emerged from the car and they were talking to one another, but he couldn't hear what they were saying.

'Can you tell us your name, please?'

'Andrew Spruce,' he said. He told himself he'd done nothing wrong, that this was preposterous. He hadn't set foot inside the school gates.

'Do you have a licence or some other form of identification with you?' The female officer was wearing thick black lace-up boots, a style that had been popular recently in Berlin. The gun in her holster was close; he could have reached out, unclipped it and taken it in his hands. He took his wallet from his back pocket and fumbled for his licence.

'Your licence has expired, sir,' the police officer observed.

'I'm living in Berlin. I'm just back for a week.'

'Are you staying at the address on this licence?'

He nodded.

She carried his licence back to the police car.

'Okay,' she said when she returned. 'You're not on our sex offenders register.'

Andrew cleared his throat. Something must have changed about him. It had happened gradually since he moved past the age of thirty. People had stopped giving him the benefit of their doubt. And now he seemed to be regarded as a potential threat. This is what had happened to him as he'd aged, the light illuminated him in a different way. It became less kind.

'Are you on your way home?'

He nodded. He felt exhausted, suddenly overcome with jet lag and fatigue.

The female officer's face softened with a sudden rush of sympathy. 'Do you need a lift somewhere?' she asked.

'Could you take me home? To the address on my licence?'

The female officer looked at the man standing beside the car. He nodded.

When the police car pulled up, his mother emerged from the house.

'Andy,' she said. Her voice was high and unsteady.

He thought the situation might have even been funny now, being brought home by the police as an adult. That this might finally make up for his unremarkable years as a teenager when his peers were staying out all night partying and he spent his time in the darkroom alone sluicing photographic paper in shallow basins of fluid.

'In future, try to avoid the school grounds,' the male officer said as he followed his mother inside.

9

The next day he decided to go to Rushcutters Bay, to see again the apartment he had shared with Kirsten for two years. He caught the bus into the city and walked down William Street, a noisy, overwhelming thoroughfare. It had been raining earlier that morning and the cement and bitumen were wet. As he approached the building, there was a heavy feeling in his gut. He remembered that feeling from when he'd lived there with Kirsten, the conflict between the desire he felt for her and the need to have his own space. He loved her, but her way of returning his love was to need him.

The apartment block was built of dark red bricks with windows facing onto New South Head Road, where the traffic tore down the hill and off to the east. Their apartment had one small bedroom and their windows were in shadow for most of the day. It was so dark inside that they always had to have a light turned on, even in summer. The carpet was worn, with strange ambiguous stains left by those who had lived there before. The bathroom was the only room in the apartment that had been renovated, as though the owner had started the process but hadn't followed through. Sometimes he had stood in the shower with the door closed; it was the only place he felt he had any privacy when Kirsten was also home. The sound of the stream of water hitting the recess around him had washed away the other noises of the apartment. He could almost pretend to himself he was alone.

Their furniture was mismatched and everything they owned had been given to them or was on loan. On the dining table they had set up their computers, one at each end, and they had sat there together, working on assignments, one of them getting up occasionally to make a fresh pot of tea. Their bed was behind a curtain, clothes were flung across the room. Their wardrobe was an open rack. Everything they owned was exposed and neither of them could keep anything to themselves. It was no way to live with another person; he knew that now. But in their youth and inexperience, they had thought this was what sharing a life entailed. In those first six months of living together, he would have given everything he had to her, without understanding what the consequences of doing so would have been. Thinking of that space now, a warmth passed through him, a memory that felt claustrophobic; it was a place where emotions had started off pleasant but had soured.

There was a day he remembered well, although the memory seemed faded, the colour drained from the scenes. He had been out all day, working in the studio on his major work, due at the end of that semester. Sometimes he slept in the studio for a few hours, woke and kept working, staying there through the night. He wasn't sure where he got the motivation from and sometimes his interest in photography felt closer to an obsession.

He had come home one afternoon around five. It was late in the year, the air was warm, familiar, with the sense that things were ending. The apartment was still when he opened the door. The air was suddenly cold and he heard a deep-throated grumble, the beginning of a storm. He saw a bowl and a mug in the kitchen from when Kirsten ate breakfast before she left for work that morning. He washed them under the tap. From their apartment, they could sometimes hear noise from the stadium in Moore Park and there must have been a football game on, because the surge of voices drifted towards him, a chorus of exaltations.

He enjoyed those moments of solitude. Outside the traffic moved in bursts, the sound of it reaching him, the buses and trucks through his window like the groans and complaints of people he didn't know, plaintive, full of sorrow and anger. The gruff exhale of a truck as it shifted down a gear. This was what he loved, this making sense of the world. When he was alone like this, the world could mutate and change; it could become what he imagined it to be.

Fat voluptuous clouds scudded low in the sky. The shadows had become thin, disappearing slowly in anticipation of rain. An old skip sat on the side of the road. Someone had moved out of an apartment in their building and deposited the refuse of their life into the metal bin. There was a plastic doll with its arm missing, its hair teased out. He could have stood there forever at that window, from where he could see the world but it couldn't touch him.

He moved into the bedroom, where the room smelt of their bodies from the stale sheets. From the rack, he took a fresh shirt off a hanger. He had been wearing the same clothes for two days. That was when he noticed the shape on the bed. Kirsten was lying there. He moved around to her side of the bed and watched her for a moment.

She was beautiful and still. The sheets followed the contour of her body. In her silence she was perfect. He found himself thinking what a fine photograph this would make: Kirsten lying in bed with the sheets wound around her. He thought of his camera in his bag in the lounge room. It was the moment he realised that he saw the world in terms that could be framed.

Her arms were flung up over her head, the way she often slept at night, and as he watched he noticed that along her arms were long red marks, scratches with a thin line of blood, like lines drawn with a felt-tip pen. They were evenly spaced along the inside of her arms, from her wrists to her elbows and up into her armpits. It was the first time he noticed these wounds. She lay there unmoving, the expression on her face soft and contented.

He picked up the clothes strewn across the floor, thinking it would be a good time to put on a load of laundry, when the communal machines weren't often in use.

As he was loading the clothes into the machine, the rain broke, big tropical beads of water scattered over the roads outside, bouncing like glass beads. The rain hit the windows in a chorus of drums.

He returned to their bedroom and saw Kirsten stir. A twitch of her foot and then the movement of an arm as she rolled to her side.

'Are you awake?' he asked.

She sat up and there was an expression on her face, first of disorientation and then of panic.

'It's only just after five. Didn't you go to work today?' He's not proud of the fact that, when he was living with her, he couldn't always find it in himself to be kind to her.

She rubbed her head. 'Migraine,' she said.

'Oh, okay. I stayed at the studio last night. I was working. Sorry I didn't call.'

'You didn't call?' she said, rubbing the side of her face with her hand.

He shook his head. She lay back down. He went to the kitchen to make himself a cup of sweet, milky tea. When he came back into the room later, she'd fallen asleep again. The rain outside stopped suddenly. Its noise ceased at once, subsiding like the passing of a violent temper.

He went out that night, to the bar near his art college, with some friends in his year. When he came home, Kirsten was awake, watching television in the dark. The television light hit her face.

'You're still up?' he asked.

She nodded. 'I'm not tired now. I slept too long in the afternoon.'

He sat down beside her on the couch. She was wearing a long-sleeved shirt. She put her arm around him and he flinched.

He moved back to his mother's house the following week.

•

He stood looking at the apartment block. Sweat prickled on his palms. She'd kept doing it, too, making those marks on her arms. After they stopped living together, they were more frequent and deeper and when they healed, they became thin white scars. He knew he should have said something to Kirsten about it, but he didn't know how to deal with the immensity of what was wrong in her life.

He rubbed his arms as though something unpleasant had settled on his skin. He wanted to be away from there; his limbs were loose with a sudden desire to flee. He walked back up the hill towards Kings Cross, away from that terrible memory, over the footbridge, up the hill and down Darlinghurst Road to Oxford Street. This strip of road was so well known to him that walking down it now, after he'd just been to visit the old place, seemed hyperreal to him, a sequence taken from a recurring dream. As he walked, he felt a separation from the world, one so definite it might have run along a perforated seam.

This discomfort he felt could be cured only by taking photographs, though he had nothing now to photograph. He'd heard nothing from the girl he saw in Leichhardt and most of his equipment was still in Berlin. He felt a flicker of anxiety as he thought of his lights and screens, these things that were so essential to him in the darkness of winter while he stood in a world washed with light.

He passed a butcher's shop, and his eye was caught by the careful arrangement of the meat in the window, the glossy shades of red and pink. He stopped and stared. Different sorts of meat had different shades, the pork cutlets were a weak pink, the steak blue-red and trimmed with a rind of fat. The chicken breasts appeared slightly grey. At the back of the display, almost hidden, he saw a silvery mass of offal, jumbled and formless shapes. It was impossible to tell what it might have once been. He touched the glass and the butcher frowned at him. He wore a white apron with red stains smeared across his thighs where he wiped his hands clean.

He walked inside to buy a leg of lamb to cook for his mother for dinner. As he stood at the counter, he peered into the coolroom and saw carcasses hanging inside from hooks, skinned and vulnerable, their heads and feet removed, legs out in front of them as though to protect them from a fall.

10

On Wednesday he emerged from his bedroom at ten, managing somehow to have slept for eleven hours. When he entered the lounge room, he saw through the open bench his mother was at the kitchen sink, washing up plates. The gloves she wore were pink like irritated skin. He rubbed his face with his hands.

'Good morning,' she said. 'Sleep well?'

He nodded. His mother shook bubbles from the dishes and stacked them in the rack. He still hadn't told his mother about Kirsten. But his mother had known Kirsten and she would have to be told.

'Mum, there's something you should know.'

His mother turned around slowly and looked at him and for a moment, as her gaze struck his, he had the impression that she thought he was about to accuse her of something. He shifted his eyes to the floorboards; they were old and in places the varnish was gone and soft, raw wood remained. His father's bare feet had touched that wood, he thought sadly, before he looked back up at his mother. There were traces of his father everywhere in this house, in this city.

On the calendar his mother kept on the fridge, he saw that it was already the second week of February and his return flight was at the end of the week. The days were moving impossibly quickly and he felt he'd achieved nothing since he came back.

He took a deep breath before he spoke.

'Do you remember Kirsten Rothwell? Had you been in touch with her recently?' He wasn't sure why, but when they were together his mother befriended Kirsten; the two of them talked on the telephone, sometimes they met for coffee. His mother never spoke about Kirsten to him, but every time they met in his absence he felt slighted.

'No, I haven't heard from Kirsten in years. Not since before you left for Berlin. Why?'

'She disappeared. Near Lake George. They think she may have drowned.'

'Oh my god,' his mother said and covered her mouth with a gloved hand. She closed her eyes. When she opened them, she looked at him with a different set of eyes. 'What happened?'

'I don't know very much about it. Stewart sent me an email to tell me when I was in Berlin.'

'God, that's just—it's terrible,' she said.

'Yes,' he said, 'it is.' He was aware of the inadequacy of his own words.

His mother's body slumped. 'So is this why you've come back? Is it to do with Kirsten?'

He didn't want to answer her. He nodded and worried he might cry. She turned back around and continued with the dishes. In her reflection in the window, he could see her lips pressed firmly together. The mention of death had this effect on her. They could not speak of death in this house without it being a reference to the one that defined them.

He turned to go back to his bedroom then stopped. He was back in Sydney to confront the truth about Kirsten but suddenly he felt compelled to confront other truths too. Another person he had loved had died and now a need to know everything rose in him.

How many times, as a boy, had he been on the verge of asking? At night when they'd finished their evening meals, in the car after school or on the way to his aunt's house in the mountains. He'd look away from her and resolve to ask, but then when he turned back towards her he wouldn't say a word. He was too aware that he might hurt her. Somehow, he'd always lacked the courage, placing her need for silence above his own need for knowledge.

'Mum,' he said now.

She turned around.

'How did he die?' Speaking the words, he felt as though he was pushing through a false wall.

She looked up at him, her face turned smooth and white. 'You mean your father?'

'Yes, I mean Dad.'

'I never told you?' she said softly, shaking her head, as though unable to believe this oversight. Her features looked heavy. She removed her gloves and moved closer to him.

'It was an aneurysm. In his brain.'

'I'd always assumed it was a heart attack.' He couldn't believe that he'd lived under that misapprehension for the past twenty-five years. All his life he'd felt ashamed for not knowing and now he felt embarrassed for not having asked sooner.

'Oh, Andrew. I'm sorry. It was so difficult for me to talk about it. Most of the time I felt I was barely coping myself.' His mother was staring at the wall as she spoke.

She moved to the couch and sat down. 'Maybe we should talk about it now? I know it was a long time ago, but do you think it would be useful?' She looked tired. His mother's words seemed to be floating, light and full of air, drifting towards him like paper lanterns.

His father had died twenty-five years ago and these were the first words she'd spoken to him about it. She opened her mouth to speak again and an impulse passed through him, a need to be away from her.

'I should have been more open with you. I worry now. You were such a quiet child, afterwards.' Her voice was soft. 'It was my fault, the way you were. I know you felt like you never fitted in. You were so lonely. So often I think about you as a teenager and I worry that I did that to you.'

Her words settled in his bones, sharp and new like fishing hooks. What disturbed him wasn't this information about the way his father had died, so much as that he had never known the truth of it and he felt ashamed for never having had the courage to ask. He could tell from the way his mother looked at him that she was seeking his forgiveness. But he couldn't forgive her; he left the lounge room and walked down the hallway and out into the day.

Outside, walking the streets, he knew that to other people he looked like a man on the cusp of middle age, but inside he still felt small and folded up inside himself like a young boy.

11

Later, when he returned to the house, he decided he would pack and return to Berlin straight away. Berlin was where his life was now. Whatever happened to Kirsten, it wasn't worth risking his relationship with Dom to find out. He knew how his father had died and that, at least, was something. Maybe it was enough.

He lifted his suitcase, pushing his knee into it, and manoeuvred it onto the bed. He took his t-shirts from the drawer in the wardrobe and pushed them into the corner of his case. He stood in front of his wardrobe. At one end, pushed almost from sight, hung a few of his father's old business shirts on wire hangers. His mother had kept them for him, unable in her thrift to throw them all away. Perhaps she even hoped that one day he would take the sort of job his father had. Looking back, the conviction he had about photography still surprised him.

His father had worked in a bank. Before his death, he managed the branch in Leichhardt. Andrew wondered what sort of existence his father had led, going to the same place each day and attending to the same tasks, assessing loan applications, reconciling accounts and counting money. What pleasure had it given his father, that life of repetition and serving others? And what would his father make of his son's life now, this strange existence he lived, plucking ideas from the air and setting them down in pictures? Everything he did was so bound up in himself.

He laid one of his father's shirts over his arm. It had lost its stiffness, its fibres worn with age. There was a small hole above the chest pocket that might have been the nibble of a hungry moth. He moved his hand inside the shirt, the tip of his finger visible through the small opening in the fabric. The shirt was already decaying, although his memories of his father were not.

He rehung the shirt in the wardrobe and walked out into the lounge room. In the backyard was the vegetable garden his father had built and tended. His father died alone out there. It was also out there one golden afternoon that his father had given him his first camera, a birthday present, when he'd turned ten. He would always remember the texture of that fading day, how the shadows swept along the grass and the diminishing light made the world tilt. He must have known the significance of the occasion, even as it happened, because his memory of it was still strong.

His father handed him the camera.

'What is it?' Andrew said, although he knew what it was; he just wasn't sure why his father was giving it away.

'It's a camera. My old camera. I hardly use it now. I thought you might like to have it.'

It was a Rolleiflex, quite different to the point-and-shoot camera with which they took their family photographs. This black box, with its two lenses, looked more scientific with all its dials and notches. He took it in his hands, afraid that he might drop it, that he might spoil this moment of connection between him and his father.

They went out onto the front step and as he looked through the viewfinder his father showed him how the needle at the side of the frame measured the light. In the last hours of the day's sun, the needle bounced up. He twisted the lens and talked about focus, something it would take Andrew years to understand properly. It was an old camera—even for its time it wasn't a particularly sophisticated device—but the only thing that mattered to him, then and now, was that it had been given to him by his father.

'I loved taking photographs, when I was younger. I used to take a lot of photos. I even had one published in a magazine once.' His father smiled weakly, almost as though he was embarrassed to admit it now. It sounded impressive to Andrew and even then he had the idea that one day he would also like to publish a photograph in a magazine. His father rubbed Andrew's back. It meant that the lesson was over, but he didn't want this intimate discussion with his father to end. The opportunities he'd had to be this close and quiet with his dad were rare. His father was busy, often withdrawn and distracted by work.

'What sort of photograph was it?'

'It was a photo I took when we went to Tasmania, before you were born. It was a picture of an uprooted tree.'

Andrew looked at the camera and suddenly felt he was taking something important from his father and immediately wanted to give it back. 'Why don't you keep it then?' he said, and his voice was small. He held the camera out.

His father looked down as though in that instant he had seen something new in his own son. For a moment, he seemed to be contemplating taking the camera back, but then he shook his head.

'I don't have time anymore, mate. As you get older, it gets harder to find the time to do the things you like.' His father stood slowly from his crouched position and a knee cracked.

As the light dwindled, Andrew thought he understood his father for the first time; the man who had been opaque to him became knowable in those few brief moments of afternoon sun. Just before they went inside, he laid his hand on Andrew's shoulder gently, and Andrew turned his head and looked at his father's long fingers and then up into his face. He seemed gaunt, the skin following the contours of his skull.

There was something about the way his father had looked at him. As though, in that moment, as he looked at Andrew, he'd realised that one day his life would end. What he saw on his father's face that afternoon was something beautiful, a longing for his younger self unfurling across it like a great and heavy pain.

Later, Andrew had tried to capture that look on other people's faces, in photographs he had taken. Sometimes he thought this pathos was what he sought in every photograph he ever took.

•

He walked back into his bedroom, opened his suitcase and placed his folded shirts inside, but his movements gradually slowed. He thought about Kirsten and her soundless exit from the world. If he didn't find out about it now, the same thing would happen with Kirsten's death as had happened with his father's. He would never know and there would be no-one he could ask.

He pictured her walking across a flat landscape towards a silvery lake and disappearing into water. He had done nothing, really, to find out more about it. He'd made no real effort to contact her family. Maybe the truth was he didn't want to know. His bed gave beneath him as he lay down on it. Through the mattress, he felt a few tight springs in his back. Maybe he was afraid of knowing.

He decided he should at least contact Kirsten's mother before he returned to Berlin. If he didn't do it now, he would have to live with not knowing and there'd already been too much of that in his life. He'd call Stewart and ask if Louise had Kirsten's mother's phone number.

•

Later that night, as his mother slept, he called Dom again. He tried to corral his thoughts, to concentrate on what he would say to her. He wanted to tell her, finally, how his father had died. He thought she would be pleased with him for finding out. But how could he tell her now, about his mother's silence, that they'd never spoken about his father's death? That he had been left to reconstruct the details of it for himself and never dared to ask?

He took the phone out to the back veranda. The plastic felt brittle in his hands, too flimsy to receive such serious news.

'*Hallo?*' Dom said, answering her phone against a background of clatter. He heard the sudden racket of the train. '*Wie bitte?*' She mustn't have heard his voice properly.

'It's me—Andrew,' he said, feeling he had to yell to make himself heard above the background noise.

'Andrew?' Her voice seemed to drift, as though she was speaking over wind.

'Yeah. I'm still in Sydney.' His voice was loud and earnest. Outside the night sky was not black but blue, illuminated by the glow of the city beneath it.

There was a surge of noise across the line. 'I'm sorry, what was that?'

'Nothing. I just wanted to say hi,' he said, loudly and slowly. The sound through the phone alternated between static and silence.

'You're going to be back in Berlin next week, right?' Her voice echoed as though she was speaking through a tin can.

'Yes, I'm coming back,' he said. 'But I still haven't spoken to Kirsten's parents. I'm going to see if I can contact them tomorrow.' He heard his voice as he spoke and it sounded foreign to him. There was a note of falseness to it, the voice of a person trying to convince himself as he spoke. 'I just need to find out more about it.' He had the sudden feeling of speaking from outer space, floating there alone, his voice bouncing between satellites, across the sky and back to her.

'Sorry, what happened? I can hardly hear you. I'm on the U-Bahn. It's snowing heavily here and I'm on my way to class. You'll be back the day after me though, won't you? In Berlin, I mean.' Her voice climbed higher.

He thought of her in her jeans, with her long black boots pulled up over them, her cloche hat and long green coat. He loved that image of her, walking carefully across the snow, the crunch of it beneath her, a sound like finely ground glass.

'Yes, I think so. I guess it depends. Also, I might be able to take some photos for the exhibition while I'm here—of a young girl I found a few days ago.' His voice had grown unsteady. He hadn't heard from the girl's mother and he wouldn't in any case have time over the next few days. If she did get in touch with him, he might have to delay his flight.

'Can you call me back later so we can talk? I can't hear you properly at the moment.'

'Okay,' he said. 'I'll call back in a few hours.' He waited for her reply, but she was already gone.

By the time he called back, he'd lost the nerve to speak about his father's death; instead he let the conversation drift towards easier things. They spoke about her classes in Cologne, the students she was growing attached to and he was so happy to speak to her about comfortable things, he didn't raise the possibility of delaying his return flight.

12

Even after he and Kirsten broke up, he'd continued to sleep with her for almost ten years. To other people they were no longer a couple, but in secret they continued to share their bodies at night.

There was a comfort in the sex they had together afterwards and it was sex without emotion. The longer it continued, the more it became about their simple, physical needs and in the end, before he left for Berlin, it became sex that admitted its own violence. He craved it, and no other encounter during that time satisfied him sexually. The feeling he had when he was inside her was one that sat close to anger, as though he was frustrated that his attraction towards her continued.

At this time, what passed between them was much

darker, with a coarser and more manipulative intent. The stakes were higher after they'd separated, their feelings exposed and unprotected. What they felt could no longer be discussed and, in order to keep seeing each other, it could surface only in their brief and urgent acts of sex. He knew it was unhealthy, but he still felt drawn to Kirsten.

They both saw other people. They spoke on the phone from time to time and she would say things, small suggestions that might have meant nothing, but he knew her well enough to know that her words were baited hooks.

'I just got out of the shower,' she would say. If he called her at night, she would speak breathlessly. Or she would talk about a man she worked with, her words slow and heavy. Sometimes, if he left her a message, she'd call him back and say, 'I've been out,' her words elusive, hinting at something, designed to provoke jealousy in him, but all he felt was sadness.

Sometimes she would arrive at his apartment in the middle of the night, drunk. Often he was already asleep and he woke to the abrupt buzz of his intercom. He'd stand at the door of his apartment in his underwear to let her in and they'd both collapsed into his bed together. Those nights weren't even about sex. They simply held each other and the smell of alcohol from her breath filled his apartment as they slept.

The marks on her arms persisted; they became thicker and more pronounced, noticeable at a casual glance.

'Kirsten, what is this?' he said one night, holding her arm up to the bedside light.

She tugged her hand back and rolled over away from the light.

'Sometimes I worry about you,' he said to her back. Her singlet was twisted across her shoulders.

She didn't reply and stayed facing the wall. That night she left while he was asleep and he didn't see her again for months. It troubled him that this was the only way Kirsten had found to express her feelings, the only outlet for her pain. He tried to encourage her to draw again, but she said she'd lost interest in it or that she was too out of practice to start again.

They kept seeing each other this way until he found himself in his early thirties without a stable relationship and still tied to Kirsten. For many years he wanted to end it, but then he would have to face the reality of confronting his mid-thirties alone in the world. And in truth, though she was difficult, he cared too much about her to hurt her.

•

The last time he saw her—not long before he left for Berlin—they'd met for dinner in a Thai restaurant in Newtown. He got off the bus on the other side of the street and as he stood at the lights, waiting for them to change, he saw Kirsten through the restaurant window. King Street was congested with cars, buses and bikes weaving in and out of traffic, exhaust fumes making everything appear dirty and used. Behind the glass Kirsten looked still; her only movement was to lift a small porcelain teacup and hold it to her mouth as she took a sip. From that distance, her skin was white and waxy, and as he watched her, he thought of a woman in an old Dutch painting, the expression on her face, the look of uncertainty about what she was doing there and the melancholy that clings to a person who does not know they are being observed. There was a ghostliness about her as she sat behind glass. Seeing her there, he felt a brief stab of regret that he was leaving for Berlin soon.

On entering the restaurant, he'd stooped down and kissed her on the cheek. She leant in towards him and pressed her cold cheek against his. There was a sickly comfort to the feeling, as though he was performing a habit he'd already outgrown. He sat down and poured himself a cup of tea from the warm pot on the table and the smell of jasmine rose from the steam. When the waitress arrived at their table, he ordered pad see ew with extra chilli. He liked that type of food, chilli, ginger and lemongrass, flavours that made his whole head tingle.

Normally when she saw him, Kirsten asked what he was working on, about his exhibitions and what he'd seen in the places he'd travelled to since they'd last met, but that night something had changed. She sat opposite him stiffly, her smiles small and compressed. After they'd ordered he asked, 'So, how's work?'

Kirsten never had resumed her degree. She deferred and deferred and finally withdrew. All he knew about her job was that it was essentially administration. She typed and she answered phones. She worked for a barrister in the city and earned more than Andrew did. He couldn't understand it, this impulse she had to give up on herself before she'd really started.

'Oh, fine. I'm fine.'

'That's great. Getting some drawing done?' Kirsten had that rare and unusual thing, exceptional natural talent. Many people have some level of ability, something that could be worked on and developed, but she had a gift. All he did was point a camera and take a shot, his art was produced by an act that was essentially mechanical. His only skill was in finding the right subject, of being able to look at a person and know what they would look like framed.

Her mouth formed a hard shape. 'No, I hardly draw these days. To be honest, I don't have time anymore, working full time.'

'Then you should make time.'

'Why bother? Why struggle for years and years to get nowhere? And it becomes too hard. I mean, it starts off and I'm enthusiastic about the work, but then to get it right becomes such a chore.'

'Well, you definitely won't succeed with that attitude.' He noticed, suddenly, that the restaurant around them had become too loud. The group beside them seemed to be yelling, their laughter pealed down the table like screams. The waitress placed their meals on the table. The broccoli was a sharp green, the sliced red chillies on top scattered seeds over his noodles.

When he looked up again, Kirsten's eyes were focused on him and there was a sharpness in them that he hadn't seen before.

'So, have you found any more *strange* people to photograph?' Her words were small and sharp, aimed at him like darts.

He bit into a chilli, coughed and reached for his glass of water.

'Strange people?' he tried to say, but his voice was weak and tears streamed down his face.

'That's your thing, isn't it? That's what you do. You find someone who has something wrong with them and you take their photograph.' Her mouth was small and punishing.

He pressed a paper napkin to his eyes to stop them from watering. He continued eating his noodles, forcing himself to finish what was on his plate, as though not finishing might amount to some concession of defeat. She was being cruel to him and it wasn't the first time. Sometimes he thought she enjoyed this power she had over him; other times he wondered if he derived some secret pleasure from her cruelty too. Maybe he even believed he deserved it, because he wasn't able to give her what she wanted from him: a normal, domestic life.

And at some level, he knew Kirsten was right. He photographed other people's faces and traded off them. It was a background worry he always had about his work—that he was seeking out people who were in some way damaged and exposing them to light. All of his successes, he felt, owed more to his subjects than to his skill.

They ate the rest of their meal in silence and when they were out on King Street, he felt his whole face throb with heat. Kirsten waved at him, took a step back and left him alone on the footpath. He never told her he was leaving for Berlin and he'd never heard a word from her again. He had wanted to help Kirsten and the fact that he was unable to made him feel he had failed her.

13

As he lay in bed the next morning, he heard the phone ring and he thought for a moment about leaving it, letting it ring out and transfer through to voicemail. In the mornings after he woke, it always took him some time to warm to the world. But not many people had his telephone number here and it could be Dom calling. He threw off the covers and rummaged through his bag for his phone.

'Hello?'

'Hi, my name is Pippa Davis. I, um, looked you up?'

He didn't immediately recognise the voice.

'Pardon?' He looked back at his bed longingly. The sheets looked soft and inviting.

'You wanted to photograph my daughter? We met outside her school last Friday?'

'Oh, yes. I remember now. Sorry.' The memory of the girl with the lopsided face returned to him. The thought of her produced a shudder of recognition, that he often had when he identified the future subjects of his work.

'I looked up your website. Your photographs are—' she hesitated '—beautiful.'

'Beautiful?' he said. There was something about him, some small fault in the way he was wired, that made him more comfortable with criticism than with praise. No matter how much experience he'd had, how detached and professional he could make himself sound, his photographs always made him feel awkward. Seeing his own work was like looking at his reflection—all he saw were the faults, the things he thought could be better.

'Maybe *truthful* is a better word,' she said after a pause, and he felt more comfortable with that appraisal. 'I'm still not entirely comfortable, though. I just worry about Phoebe and the way she looks. Sometimes I think she doesn't understand how different she is to other people. I'm not sure photographing her is such a good idea.' She sighed. 'But Phoebe wants to do it. She's at that age, I guess. She's curious about her own looks.'

'I've photographed many children her age. I try to involve them as much as possible in the process. Most of my models enjoy being involved.' Listening to himself speak, he sounded like a salesman reeling off a pitch.

'But Phoebe is different to most children,' she said.

'Because of her face.' She cleared her throat. 'Is that why you want to photograph her, because of her face?'

'Well, yes, I guess it is.' He wasn't used to being asked questions so directly. 'But it's not the only reason.'

'What do you mean?' Pippa asked cautiously.

'I mean, it is her face. I don't know how to explain it.' He thought for a moment, wondering how to express his meaning. 'Her face lets you see inside her.'

'Oh, I see.' She was silent for a moment and he thought he might have offended her. He felt relieved when she spoke again. 'Well, what is it you had in mind?' she asked.

'I probably need her in the studio for a day or two. I usually rent a studio space in Chippendale.' He wondered if the same studio would still be available.

'I mean, what do you intend for the photos of Phoebe? We've never been involved in anything like this before.'

It always sounded strange, whenever he tried to explain his work to other people, and it rarely made any sense to him until it was finished. He thought of the girl's face, tugged at on one side, how he'd seen her in the playground in the late afternoon light and immediately knew he wanted to take her photograph without really understanding why. He could already tell, just from watching her in those moments, that she was too self-aware to be photogenic; she seemed almost to wince at the world. The way she held on to the broken hat carefully but firmly, not as though it was something damaged, but as though it was something that still needed to be taken care of.

'It would be a fairly simple photograph,' he said. 'The important part will be getting the details of the shot right, the lighting and so forth.'

'Oh,' she said, sounding unsure what to make of his answer. 'Well, if you do photograph her, I would want to be there. I mean, I feel I would need to be present. Photographs like yours—they take people and preserve them and that is something my daughter will have to live with for the rest of her life.'

Nobody had ever said anything like that to him before. Sometimes people said *no*, but usually the idea of being photographed for art was too alluring to resist. The idea of being captured on film was seductive; people usually associated photography with beauty.

'Well, I can let you see the images before they're exhibited and you can certainly be there while I'm taking them.' He heard the sound of a bus outside, easing away from the stop, the breath of its brakes.

'What if Phoebe and I don't like the photos? Will you exhibit them even if we aren't happy with them?'

He had never given another person control over his own work and he reacted badly to suggestions from galleries, turning his back on their comments. It was his work, he always felt, and if it succeeded or failed, it ought to be on the basis of his own choices. But it was also Phoebe's face and she was a child. 'Well, if there's something you seriously object to, I'll definitely consider your opinion, but usually I ask people to sign a consent form before I take the photograph.'

'No, I think I would want to have the right to say "no", especially if Phoebe changes her mind,' she said firmly.

This was getting more complicated than he'd intended. He knew it would probably be best not to proceed, to wait until he was back in Berlin and find another subject to photograph there. But instead he heard himself saying, 'Well, okay. If Phoebe is unhappy with the image, I will agree not to exhibit it.' The shoot wouldn't be too expensive, he reasoned, and it would be worth taking the risk, as long as he could get it done quickly. He had a feeling about Phoebe; this could be the photograph he'd been searching for, the one that would make the impact he needed.

'Okay, that sounds reasonable. When were you thinking?'

'Are you available in the next few days?' He still hoped he could take the photographs and fly back to Berlin without changing his flights, but the timing would be tight.

'I'm working tomorrow and the next day; I work at the library in Leichhardt. And the weekend might be difficult anyway, but what about Monday and Tuesday next week. Could we do it then?'

On Saturday he was due to fly back to Berlin. To take this girl's photograph, he would have to delay his return flight. He bit his cheek and thought of Dom. He wasn't sure how he would explain this to her without upsetting her more than he already had.

'All right,' he said, after a pause. 'Yes, I'll check if I can hire a studio then.'

When he hung up, he stared at his phone. He thought of the photograph he was most recognised for, the photo that Pippa would have seen when she searched his name online. It seemed a sort of magic to him now, after years of trying to get his work exhibited, how quickly it had happened.

He was out to dinner with friends one night when one of them mentioned a man he had been to school with who had never lost his set of baby teeth. He knew immediately that he wanted to photograph him.

Andrew rented a warehouse in Redfern for the day, the cheapest studio he could find; the space had once been a mechanic's garage and there were still oil stains on the dusty cement floor and a smell of metal. When the man walked into his studio that day, he seemed stern, with a hard face, his handshake brief and his palm rough. He was a large man, and he stood with his feet apart, as though to distribute his weight evenly. Later, when the man laughed, his laugh was loud. It boiled through his body and filled the room. It was difficult to reconcile the sudden rush of happiness contained in that laugh with the sombre man who had first greeted him. Andrew understood then that he was a man who, because of his appearance, treated the world with a certain suspicion, but underneath was otherwise happy.

It was a summer day and in the heat inside the warehouse, he felt himself slowly baking. The fan did nothing but stir up hot and stale air. They'd been in the studio for five hours and he was sweating, his clothes touching his body like clammy hands.

He opened a window to let the air in and when he was back in front of the camera, the man yawned and he had glimpsed something, maybe it was a brief glimpse into his own future, and he took the photo. He pressed the camera shutter down so hard his finger hurt afterwards. Inside the man's mouth was pink and damp and it took up almost the whole frame of the shot, so that Andrew might have been looking into the mouth of a lion. At the corner of one eye was a tear, a small, perfect droplet; in the photo it almost looked like a small diamond. When it was exhibited later, he called the photo *Teething* and with that image his life was changed.

Afterwards, he found a gallery in Sydney to represent him. Until then, he'd mostly had only group shows and his chief success had been a shortlisting for a photography award many years before. He'd had one solo show at a co-op gallery in Surry Hills where he hadn't even sold enough prints to recoup his own costs. But after *Teething* he was no longer dependent for his income on taking pictures of things he didn't want to photograph, like furniture, food and underfed women in expensive clothes. The realm of commercial photography was behind him, its smallness and falseness no longer concerned him.

The next year the photograph had been exhibited as part of a group show in the Centre Pompidou in Paris and afterwards his photographs had been acquired by museums all over the world. And even though he still suffered setbacks and his existence was never extravagant, he could work quietly by himself from then on, pursuing only the things that mattered to him, working with ideas and subjects that he felt brought him some truth.

More recently, he wondered if his career would forever be defined by that single moment in time. Nothing he had created since had quite lived up to it—at least, not in his own mind. No other work he created had ever felt as clean. Sometimes, he felt he existed in the shadow of that photograph. No other picture had ever come to him so easily.

14

Andrew called his real estate agent and asked if they'd found new tenants for his apartment in Darlinghurst, thinking that if they hadn't he could stay there himself for a few days before he flew back to Berlin. It was difficult too, for him to live so close to his mother after her disclosure; his anger at her silence flared each time he saw her. He'd bought his apartment with the money that had been put aside for him out of his father's life insurance policy; the amount of money had slowly grown with him as he aged. By the time he was twenty-seven, he had just enough to buy a small studio apartment in an old building not far from where he had once lived with Kirsten. He'd managed to buy it before the property market in Sydney boomed a few years later. Now it was worth double what he paid for it—it was his one piece of financial security in a life characterised by taking risks. He'd never renovated it and the low rent generally attracted students and short-term tenants.

When the agent said it hadn't been let, he asked her to wait a week or two before advertising it again.

When he ended the call, his thoughts careened towards Dom. Now that he had definitely decided to stay a few extra days in Sydney, he couldn't put off telling her any longer.

In the corner of his mother's lounge room, the television flickered on mute; the afternoon movie was about to start.

He dialled Dom's number. It seemed to take an impossibly long time to connect.

'*Hallo?*'

'Dom?'

She hesitated. Or maybe it was the delay on the line. 'Andrew?'

'Sorry, did I wake you? I suppose it must be quite early there.' Hearing her voice produced a softness inside him. It cushioned his insecurities.

'Don't worry. I had to wake up for an early class anyway.'

He swallowed, not wanting to think about Dom living her life without him. He wanted her to stay immobile, like a butterfly under glass, until he was ready to return to her.

'I'm sorry. I miss you. I needed to hear your voice.' Their movements on each end of the phone echoed.

'Have you packed yet?' There was something about the way she spoke; the halting words, her accent made her sound as though she was savouring everything she said.

'Dom, I'm sorry, but I'm going to have to delay my return flight.'

'Delay it? Why? What has happened?'

'I've found a girl here I really want to photograph for the London show. She's really special—she has a very unusual face.' He was aware he was speaking too quickly.

'You've been scouting over there?' He heard in her voice that she trusted him slightly less now, that she was testing his honesty.

'No. It sort of happened by accident when I walked past my old primary school. But I can't photograph her until next week, so I'll have to stay a few extra days.'

'Okay. So when will you be back now?'

He realised he couldn't answer her. He still hadn't spoken to Kirsten's mother, though he felt he had to before he could go back to Berlin. And still he didn't want to disappoint her. He fell into happiness with Dom. It wound around him soft as cotton, without him having any real sense of it happening. Love had made him feel endless, it had lulled him into thinking it could never end.

'Soon,' he finally said. 'The photographs won't take long.'

'So another few days? A week?'

'I don't know. A week or two? The thing is, I still have to get in touch with Kirsten's mother.' He couldn't put any brakes on his words. They were moving out of his mouth and along a downhill track.

'Another *two* weeks? Why is this thing with Kirsten so important, anyway? I don't understand why you had to go back.'

'I don't know, Dom. She's an old girlfriend of mine; I feel like I owe something to her, I guess.'

'Wait, she was an old girlfriend of yours?'

Those words had slipped out, and he knew he should have told her earlier. Now it would sound like he'd been hiding it from her.

'I didn't know that. You've never even talked about your old girlfriends with me.'

'No, it was—I don't know. I should have said something.' He ran a hand over his face, realising how he had mismanaged things, though it would have cost him nothing to be open with her.

'Well, I don't know either. You tell me you don't want me there and now it's an old girlfriend of yours. Sometimes I don't understand you.' Her words hurtled towards him.

When he hung up the phone, he looked out the window and outside a storm bird called, the call that sings in rain.

•

He drove to the storage unit where his belongings were packed away in cardboard boxes, to retrieve the few things he would need for the week or two he was here. He went through them one by one, finding things in unopened boxes he hadn't seen since he moved to Berlin, digging them out like an archaeologist uncovering the traces of a former life. His old possessions now looked strange, inconsequential, objects that served no function in the life he now led. The warehouse in Waterloo was a cavernous space with high ceilings and the noises of people sorting through boxes was amplified in the space around him.

The people who went to these sorts of places were single people, as he had been when he'd left Sydney, people making decisions about the things in their lives they could live without. The warehouse was divided into rows of locked spaces, cubicles partitioned by thin walls. Some spaces were small and others were almost large enough to live inside. One man in shorts and thongs unloaded a dining table from a trailer and the chairs that went with it. Andrew remembered that feeling of packing up his life, compressing it into the space allotted to him and of leaving that day for Berlin, feeling unburdened and free. He had tricked himself into believing there were things he could leave behind, parts of himself that wouldn't travel with him. He could escape his regrets.

This was a place of transition, like a train station, a place people passed through on their way somewhere else. It had taken him a long time to understand that not all people were the way he was, that some people found the place they thought they belonged, the first place they came across, and settled on it. The fact that they knew they would never leave was a source of great contentment.

He opened the box he'd dropped off last time he was here—a plastic box so the photographs held inside wouldn't deteriorate. He had forgotten about the photographs he'd taken of Dom two years earlier—he'd left the proofs here after dropping the prints at his gallery in Sydney. He still remembered that bargain he had struck with himself when he met her: that he would do whatever he could not to lose her. That was when the feeling of love he had for her was still something he was constantly aware of, before it faded into the background of his life and became something he assumed would always be there.

The pictures were taken at close range, on a long exposure. He had developed them himself at his studio in Berlin, at night in the dead of winter, fixing black plastic to the windows and taping the door closed in order to block out all the light. He had used tea as a toner and the colours were dark and caramel, almost sepia. It was as much about the process of photography as the images themselves. In them she was naked, but the way they were taken it was difficult to see which of her body parts were in the shot; they were ambiguous dark stretches of skin. There was a photo of her stomach, her navel and the skin stretched over her hip. Because of the colours and the stillness of those photographs, she might have been a sculpture in bronze. He'd brought them back to Sydney to show his gallery, but they felt the photos didn't fit with the rest of his work. They were more personal and different to his other work—there was nothing broken or damaged about Dom as there usually was with his subjects. They were a demonstration of feelings about which he had no doubt. In the end, the gallery kept only a few prints to show to select collectors.

He put the photographs back inside their plastic sleeves, because he was worried, now, that he might cry, knowing he upset the woman with whom he'd finally found a love that he could sustain. He looked up into the gaping space over this cubicle that stored all the things he owned and hadn't taken to Berlin. He felt something in his throat each time he swallowed, like a piece of broken china lodged where his Adam's apple should have been.

When he looked up again, a young boy was standing at the door of his cubicle. He was wearing yellow from his neck to his feet, a baggy outfit like a sack that was not fitted to his body. He was playing with something in his hand that was connected to a cord and he had a collar of fur around his neck. It took Andrew a moment and a tilt of his head to understand the boy was wearing a lion's suit. The boy couldn't have been much older than six or seven, but Andrew could already see in his face the trace of the adult he would become; the man he would grow into was already waiting to devour him. He found himself wanting to tell the boy to make sure he enjoyed this time he had as a child, to make sure that he was aware of it, because he couldn't know how quickly it would pass.

'Are you going away too?' the boy asked. His hair was parted to one side, brushed that way while it was still wet. Andrew could see the teeth marks where the comb had been run through his hair. His hair was the white sort of blond that cannot stay that way. When the boy moved closer to him, he smelt clean and alkaline, like soap.

Andrew shook his head. 'I live on the other side of the world. I'm only back here to visit.'

'Where do you live?' the boy said, sceptical, and he reached for the photographs of Dom in their plastic sleeves. Andrew had forgotten what it was like to be a child, to believe that all the world belonged to you.

'Berlin, in Germany,' he said. He wasn't sure he should be having this conversation with a child now. At that moment, he wasn't sure he could muster the energy he needed to be kind.

'My pop's from Germany. He was born there. He came to Australia on a boat.' This was a child's world, a world in which everything refers back to you. 'We're going to America to live. My dad's got a new job there.' He pulled the hood up over his head and there were two triangles on top with smaller, pink triangles inside. A lion's small ears. 'He doesn't know how long for, though.' He looked at Andrew uncertainly.

'That's a long way. I hope you're taking a plane?'

'I've flown before, you know.' As though the boy suspected him of assuming he had not. 'Sometimes they give you chocolate and it's in the shape of the plane,' he said and turned his head, looking at something that Andrew couldn't see from where he stood.

'Wow. I've never had chocolate like that before,' he said, taping the box of photos closed. When he looked up again, the boy had left.

He had all he needed: one saucepan, a frypan, some cutlery, a few bowls and plates. He could live this way. As it turned out, he hardly needed anything at all. He sat in his mother's car, unable to turn the key in the ignition. The car smelt of synthetic strawberry from the fragrant cardboard leaf his mother had hung from the rear-view mirror.

He was aware that he had made a decision to leave Berlin suddenly and this decision was one he now regretted. He wondered, sitting in his mother's car, whether this was why he'd taken those photographs of Dom. Whether he had known in advance that one day he might sabotage his own happiness. Maybe he didn't trust himself and he'd taken these photographs in order to be able to hold on to Dom in this one, significant way.

He drove out of the warehouse, negotiating the ramp with a thump, and he saw the boy in the lion's suit standing beside the boot of a car with a man. The boy gave him a curious look as he passed and he understood his sadness was confusing to a boy of that age. For the first time in his life, his own feelings frightened him. It was about Kirsten and now it was also about Dom. Everything he thought he knew about the world, the things he had relied on, seemed to be collapsing around him.

It rained on his way back to Leichhardt in his mother's car; the downpour was so heavy that the water sluiced across the windscreen between the strokes of the wipers. He could see the red tail-lights of the car in front of him and every time he stopped at the traffic lights, he found his eyes had filled with tears.

15

He called Stewart that afternoon. In the background was the heavy thud of a jackhammer working through cement.

'Hey, Stew, it's Andrew. How are you?'

'Andrew? Good, man, just at work.' He imagined Stewart on site, in his hard hat and business shirt.

'Just wondering if you've got time for a beer before I head back to Berlin?'

'We're busy over the weekend, mate. Could we make it next week instead?'

'Next week should be okay; I'll let you know the day. How about you come over to my apartment in Darlinghurst? I'll be there for a few days before I fly back.'

'Sure, man, sounds good.' Stewart sounded friendly but distracted, and Andrew couldn't bring himself to say that all he really wanted from Stewart were the contact details for Kirsten's parents. He didn't feel he could ask for those details over the telephone.

●

On Saturday morning, he called Pippa to find out Phoebe's dress size. That afternoon, he walked around level six at David Jones. Among the racks of small clothing, the shorts and jumpsuits in pastels for babies and primary colours for toddlers, he felt conspicuous. He felt large and grotesque, as if with every move he might be about to knock something from its place.

'Can I help you, sir?' a woman asked. She was wearing a black jacket and a pencil skirt that made her movements look restricted. Her eyebrows were drawn at two sharp angles over her eyes.

'Oh, I'm looking for a dress,' he said.

'Did you have anything particular in mind?'

'Well, I'm thinking of an off-white colour.'

'Well, let me see. How old is your daughter?'

'Oh, it's not for my daughter. But she's eleven.' His cheeks flushed with a heat that felt visible. The woman's face went blank, as though she was trying to find some other reason for him to be looking at dresses for girls. 'It's for a photo shoot. I have to take a young girl's photograph,' he said and she looked at him as though she'd just bitten into something she didn't like the taste of very much.

'I see.' She led him around the shop floor and showed him some dresses, lifting the plastic hangers from their stands and holding the dresses against her body to show him how they might look, but she turned her face away from him as she spoke. Her mouth was set in a serious line.

In the end, he settled on a cream dress with a lace collar. He thought the texture would prevent the photograph from appearing too flat. As he walked away from the counter after paying for it, he could feel the woman's eyes on him, aware that the world was less forgiving of him than it had once been, less prepared to assume his good intentions.

•

He had booked the studio for Monday and Tuesday. He woke early on Monday morning and packed his equipment into the car he had hired. The morning light was sparse and cast no shadows. At the studio, he had already set up the screen and lighting. He'd used his old lights and screens, the first equipment he'd ever owned, and the pieces had a battered look about them, scarred from overuse. The walls and floor of the room he'd hired were concrete, and the echoes of him shifting equipment returned to him off the walls. Until he had his equipment unpacked, until he had the lights arranged in the way he wanted, he could not work, he felt uneasy. When the studio was finally set up, he could believe that it might happen, that the idea he had for the photograph might become something tangible and real.

He took the parts of his camera from the case, twisting the cool metal lens until it snapped into place. His movements were quick and reflexive, like a soldier assembling a gun. He had started taking photos in quick succession, to check the lights and the set-up. It settled him, being reminded of how the camera could give attention to things, ordinary things, objects which are usually given little regard.

He set the camera up on a tripod and held the lens in his hand until he felt it turn warm. He always waited for this moment, when his camera felt like an extension of his own hands. The camera made a crunch when he pushed the button down; there was something so certain about that sound. The jolt of the flash each time he pressed the button, striking the walls with its white, sanitised light. No matter what else was happening in his life, he could always count on what the camera would do; it would always take the world, flip it upside down and restore it again the right way up on paper.

He'd asked Pippa to arrive at ten, to give him time to set up and talk to the assistant he'd hired for the day, a woman who had been recommended to him by a photographer he'd been in a group show with. He would need her to monitor the laptop for the test shots on the digital camera, changing the film in his camera, holding up light screens and moving lights. But fifteen minutes early, he heard a knock on the metal roller door to the studio, the clash of metal as the door shook in its frame.

'Hi,' Pippa said, standing with a hand on her hip, her sunglasses still covering her eyes. Pippa was not much taller than her daughter and from a distance, in a certain light, the two of them might have been sisters. Phoebe was wearing jeans, standing behind her mother, and when she emerged, he noticed something new about her, an expression that hid some submerged anger that must have been directed at him. This was the conflict people felt when they had their photograph taken: curious to see an image of themselves, yet aware that a camera isn't always kind.

'I'm afraid today and tomorrow could be very boring for you,' he said to Phoebe as he led them into the studio. 'Photography is a lot of fiddling. Taking the picture is actually the quickest part. And you should drink as much water as you can because the lights can be hot to stand under.' He unscrewed the plastic lid from a bottle of water and handed it to her. She hesitated before she took it from him.

The assistant arrived ten minutes late, a short, sturdy woman with dark hair. She was carrying a large coffee in her hand. When he shook her hand, her grip was firm. He directed her to the laptop, then produced the dress he had chosen for Phoebe. The dress had a low neckline. He had the idea that he would include her shoulders in the shot; he wanted to expose the tenderness of her young skin.

Phoebe and Pippa went to the bathroom together so Phoebe could get changed and a wave of nerves took hold of him; he was aware of how easy it would be for things to go wrong. The difference between success and failure in his profession was a very fine line.

Pippa came out first. She moved close to him and spoke in a low voice. 'So, you are going to give us the chance to look at the photographs first, aren't you? Before they're exhibited?' Her voice rose in pitch as she spoke.

He nodded. 'I can give you a week, but then I'll need to send them to my gallery. The exhibition is in March and I can't keep the gallery waiting.'

'Okay, a week should be enough time to decide.' She turned her head as Phoebe walked out of the bathroom. The girl had her hands folded over her chest.

'Is it the right size?' he asked.

'It's a bit baggy,' Pippa said, straightening the dress across Phoebe's shoulders from behind.

'That's okay, I can fix it with clips at the back,' he said.

'It looks *gay*,' Phoebe said, looking at the concrete floor with the hostility of a person who resents doing something they don't understand. In her eyes were needles of doubt.

'Phoebe!' Pippa said. 'Sorry, she picks up that sort of language from school.'

'Do you mind?' he said, moving towards her. 'I'll pull the tags off.' He placed a hand on her shoulder and felt her melt beneath him, like a small animal that offers no resistance to being held. He broke the plastic tags in his hands.

'Take a seat on the stool there if you wouldn't mind, Phoebe,' he said.

In her dress, under the lights, her limbs were pale, skinny and as supple as green wood.

'Okay, Phoebe, could you put your hands on your lap for me?' He demonstrated for her.

She arranged her hands, but she still looked prim, like someone who should have been wearing a shirt buttoned all the way up to her chin.

'I'll take a few test shots. The light will be quite bright at first.' There was a blitz from the strobe and the slow whine of the recharge. He checked the test shots on his laptop behind him.

'I need to sharpen the focus,' he said over his shoulder to the assistant, who was kneeling in front of the laptop.

He closed the aperture down and focused on Phoebe's eyes.

'Okay, looking at the floor for me,' he said. 'And push your shoulders back.'

She sat slumped, the way all self-conscious children did, defending herself against the world. Phoebe looked towards her mother and then did what he'd asked. He took a few shots that way. While he was talking to his assistant again, checking the pictures on the larger screen, Pippa had moved closer to Phoebe. He stepped back behind the camera and her presence in front of the lens sent a ripple of annoyance through him. He was so used to being in control of the situation.

'Okay, Phoebe, could you look over to the right for me? At the wall and then slowly turn your head and look at the camera.'

She looked at her mother again.

'It's okay, Phoeb,' Pippa said. He could hear the strain in her voice as she tried to sound reassuring.

When he was back behind the lens he saw again why he wanted to photograph the girl. The left side of her face drooped, as though that half of her face had been anaesthetised, but the other side of her face remained unaffected. He thought whatever it was that made her face that way must have happened when she was young, because she didn't appear to be aware of it. Her eyes were green rather than hazel, a colour without impurity, like glass held against light.

The sound of the flash recharging whined in the room, a piercing sound like a defibrillator, resonating somewhere deep in his ear. He had come to dread that sound, the sound of expectation, of the camera waiting for him to take the next photograph, for his next moment of inspiration.

It was difficult work that day. Phoebe's expression was reluctant; she looked at the camera as though she suspected it of wanting to cause her harm.

'Okay, could you just relax your face for me?' he said. When the right half of her face tensed it gave her a strange, slanted appearance. 'And look at the lens like you're looking straight through me and pretend I'm not here at all.' She smiled self-consciously. He stood and felt a twinge in his lower back. He tried not to allow his frustration to show.

'Now stand up,' he said. 'And just let your arms flop out. Shake your legs and relax. Pretend we aren't even in a studio, pretend we're at home. In your lounge room.' She smiled and looked at Pippa, who nodded.

Around twelve he stopped, clapped his hands and said, 'Okay, who's hungry? Should we go out and get some lunch?' He wanted them to eat together, to share simple food and ordinary, lunchtime conversation. He would ask Phoebe about school and try to ascertain if she had any sense of the way the world saw her. He would muster his charm and try to find some way to make her trust him.

But Pippa looked at Phoebe carefully after he spoke, as though she could see something in her that he could not, some small, invisible complaint. The silent communication that takes place between a parent and child, flowing on the currents of their moods. He thought of how his own mother knew him, but also chose not to know him, of the things she understood about him that no-one else knew and of what she wilfully overlooked.

'I think I'll take Phoebe down to Broadway. We'll get some sushi while we're there. She likes sushi. I need to buy some groceries anyway.' He took his wallet from his pocket and tried to give her some money for their lunch, but Pippa refused to take it.

He stayed at the studio and didn't eat lunch. He rarely ate when he was taking photographs, existing instead in a state of heightened anxiety. His assistant went out and came back with a sandwich.

When Phoebe and her mother came back after lunch he continued working, but by three in the afternoon, Phoebe started to yawn and slouch and he knew that he had pushed her as far as he could that day. Her posture became tight, drawing in on herself. Ordinarily this was the part of the day when his shots started to work, the models relaxed and the threat of what the camera might take from them receded to the back of their minds.

'Okay, Phoebe,' he said and stood. His lower back felt stiff and he continued to feel hunched while standing upright. 'You can get changed now. We'll start again tomorrow morning.' She stood up quickly, tugging at the dress as she moved towards the bathroom to get changed. Her sudden relief at finishing made her appear taller.

As he watched them go, part of him felt that by allowing her to leave he was giving up. He wanted to keep her there and try to extract the image he needed from her, but she was a child and he couldn't place on her the expectations he had of himself. He told the assistant she could leave for the day too, then he stayed on in the studio alone, scrolling through the photos he'd taken, but he knew he had nothing he could use. There was always this sickness at the thought that he wouldn't be able to make it work, when he had to entertain the possibility of abandoning his idea. It was a sort of floating, the feeling of returning slowly to earth from a great height, like a cinder caught in a current of cool air.

•

Outside the studio a blue light had fallen, shadows were starting to swallow the day. He walked down the lane and out onto Broadway, where the cars surged forward with the change of lights. The people walking past were young, university students, carrying books and wearing backpacks. He remembered that age and to him it didn't even seem so long ago. He had sped away from that age too quickly, without really being aware of what he was moving away from. All his life, he had been racing and it was only now he wondered what place it was he had hoped to reach so quickly.

At that age, the future had seemed large, unknown and daunting, but now it was the past that billowed up behind him, rising like a cloud of dust.

16

They arrived the next day at ten. Phoebe walked into the studio, but Pippa stood on the doorstep. She called out, 'My car wouldn't start this morning. I need to take it to a mechanic to replace the battery. Would it be okay if I left Phoebe here with you? I'll be back in an hour or two. Phoebe will be alright without me, won't she?' Her voice was high and uncertain, the in-between notes on a piano, the black keys towards the top of the scale that lingered after having been struck. She brushed a loose piece of hair from her forehead and, when she held her hands together in front of her, her fingers seemed to be shaking. Pippa looked towards his assistant for reassurance. 'I wouldn't normally leave her,' she said, looking sideways at Phoebe, 'but it's sort of an emergency.'

'Of course, she'll be fine. It will be much the same as yesterday. There's really no need for you to stay.' In fact, he would prefer it if she left, though he couldn't say so. Her absence would give him more control over the shoot.

Pippa bit her lip. 'If you're sure it's okay . . . I'll be back around lunchtime. Or maybe I should stay?' She took a step forward and he worried she was about to change her mind.

'She'll be fine,' he said.

Phoebe watched him from a distance, moving out from behind a table to a chair, always keeping something between them. She moved in front of the screen and sat down on the stool, even though he hadn't fixed the camera to the tripod yet. It was a space she knew she could occupy. She saw the dress laid over the back of the chair and moved towards it, brushing her fingers carefully across the lace.

'Yes, you can get changed into the dress again, if you like. We'll be working on the same shot as yesterday.'

She nodded and slipped her feet from her shoes, reaching for the button on her jeans. That was when he realised she was about to get changed there, in front of him and his assistant, and it provoked a sadness in him that she was so trusting, although she didn't know him at all. He was aware of how easily she could be taken advantage of.

'You remember where the bathroom is?' he said and pointed towards it.

When she came back he had the camera set up on

its tripod. There was a sudden burst of light as his assistant checked the strobes and a splinter of sound moved through the room. He smiled at Phoebe and she moved her mouth awkwardly to one side. Hers was a smile that could never look completely happy; that would, because of her face, always suggest some inner grief.

He took her photograph, but she was looking below the lens rather than into it, her gaze lowered and shy.

'Can I get you to look into the camera, Phoebe?' He was tired. He wasn't sure he was up to spending the day with her again; the thought of it exhausted him, as though the day ahead required strenuous physical activity. So often, photographing someone felt like asking them to agree to something being taken from them.

Sometimes he thought his occupation involved a sort of stealing; he stood in front of people and smiled the warm and charismatic smile of a thief and most of the time nobody noticed what they'd lost. Sometimes they didn't even understand it later, when they saw the photograph hanging on a gallery wall. And he tiptoed away afterwards with his bag of money, dressed in black from head to toe.

He asked her to sit sideways and look back at the camera and, in the first shot he took, her mouth was open, her lips moist. 'Good,' he said. 'That's great,' but as soon as he said it, she looked down.

An hour later, he remembered the biscuits he'd left, still in shopping bags from when he'd bought them the day before, on the card table he'd set up against the wall.

'Would you like a biscuit?' he said.

'What kind?' she asked, seeming uncertain about whether or not she'd heard him correctly. She looked at him cautiously, standing and moving sideways rather than towards him.

He reached into the shopping bag. 'I have fruit parcels.' He held them up. Phoebe screwed her nose up at the packet. 'And chocolate,' he said, and her eyes turned bright. As he watched her eat the biscuits, some barrier inside her seemed to go down. She ate one and then another and he wondered if she would eat the whole packet. He took one, biting off each end and prising it apart.

'You eat it like that?' Phoebe asked, still suspicious.

He nodded, feeling the chocolate clot at the back of his throat. A vacuum of feeling had ballooned open between them, created by him trying to gain her trust and her being unsure of whether to hand it over. He tried to calmly navigate his way across that space.

His assistant joined them and ate a biscuit too. She dipped hers into a cup of tea she'd made for herself and Phoebe watched as she licked the melted chocolate away. Phoebe reached for a third biscuit, picked it up, turned it over and replaced it.

'I think I'll save that one for after lunch,' she said.

'You know, you can eat as many as you like. There's a whole packet there that won't get eaten otherwise,' he said. It drew another vein of sadness from him; this restraint he saw in her that belonged to an adult. Somehow she had suppressed her child's urge to live by impulse.

When he was back behind the camera, she was more open, somehow more pliable. He'd seen this happen before; he offered a person something sweet and it made them believe he could do no wrong to them. It was a trick, a technique he had learnt, but he was never proud of himself for using it.

'Tilt your head a bit,' he said, tilting his hand to show her what he meant, and she moved her head slowly until he held his hand still to indicate where she should stop.

From then on they worked without speaking, with gestures. After about twenty minutes of working that way, she looked at him with a sudden determination. It was as if in that moment, the ambivalence she had about him faded and she decided she would no longer with-hold herself from him. She stared into the lens and a cold certainty ran through him. He didn't take his hands off the camera. He took five photographs and he knew he had what he needed from her. He turned around to his assistant who gave him a single nod of approval.

•

He had the photographs developed and scanned the next day, and the day after that he started to work on them, choosing the photos he wanted to work with first. It was hard for him to discard so many images and he kept all the photos he had ever taken on his hard drive, even those he'd never used, although he rarely went back to look at them again. Choosing one image over another always left him with a sense of loss. It was a process that felt to him like losing possibilities, which was why it always took him such a long time to decide which image to use. He liked knowing that there were so many unperfected photos still in existence, standing like shadows behind the work that was eventually exhibited.

Mostly, the work he did after taking the photograph was a process of smoothing over, of removing all the imperfections and joins, his movements small and delicate, like a potter working with clay. This was his favourite part of his work, when his view of what he had created was at its most generous, when he saw its possibilities instead of only its flaws. He made the tones more consistent, the colours starker and the contrasts sharper, moving the mouse across his computer screen in small strokes and clicks, and a sharp pain shot through his shoulder from the tension in his arm.

In photographs people were static, characterised by that single moment in time, but in real life they were more difficult to pin down. He found himself often, in conversations, wanting to tell whomever he was speaking with to stop, to be still, so he could stand back from them and take the moment he needed to understand them. In photographs, people could only ever be one thing and in the photographs he took, people became what he made them. Maybe this was why, after all, he did what he did with his life, for the feeling of distance and control he lacked in his interactions with the actual world.

He often thought his best photos were those that came out formed, that required little work and felt effortless, forged in a moment of light. It had been a long time since he'd had that, but it was how he felt about the photograph of Phoebe. There was one image in which the focus was sharp and she was looking at the camera as though she'd just lifted her eyes and the expression on her face was asymmetrical. In that shot, the texture of her skin was dewy, almost bruised with the overhead lights bearing down on her. Her eyes didn't quite focus and one turned ever so slightly out. The left side of her mouth drooped and her left eyelid was slightly closed, as though that side of her were falling asleep. He knew he had something; for the first time since *Teething*, he had produced a photograph about which he had no doubts.

•

He sent the photographs to Pippa and Phoebe in a large white envelope with cardboard behind them to prevent them from being folded in the post. He wrote a note with it, asking Pippa to let him know by the following Monday if she had any objection to the images, otherwise he would send them to his gallery.

He didn't hear back from her the next day, nor the day after that. He started to wonder whether he should use Phoebe's photograph after all. Part of him knew that he would be using Phoebe's image to further his own reputation. But when he looked at the photograph again he understood there was something about it that had to be exhibited, something that no longer belonged to Phoebe or Pippa, something that needed expressing to an audience. He hoped Pippa would see that too.

17

When he moved into his old apartment it was already mid-February and his exhibition in London was less than a month away. He found it difficult to believe that he actually used to live in that space, with the kitchen he'd always meant to renovate and the taps that dripped in the heat. The furnishings were old and worn; it felt like the apartment could never now be clean. He looked up and saw that in places, the paint was peeling from the ceiling. Out of the window the view skipped over the roofs of the Paddington terraces. It was a lonely life he had when he lived there, mostly he lived hand to mouth and he shared his existence with no-one.

He spent the years he'd lived there in his late twenties and early thirties eating tuna, instant noodles and cans of beans. Subsisting in preference to living in order to pursue a career in photography. Kirsten had been his only regular visitor. In those years he'd become a ghost of a person, giving himself to what he loved to do instead of to other people.

•

He invited Stewart over the day after the photo shoot ended. He sometimes wondered whether Stewart ever got tired of being so consistent, of always doing what was expected of him; if he had ever had the urge to do something radical, to quit his job or walk away from his marriage. To act quickly and impulsively, to risk doing something he might live to regret. But the urge that Andrew had, the need for progress, was absent in Stewart. Stewart was a man who knew how to remain steady and unchanged. It was something Andrew had once regarded with disdain, but as Stewart walked through the door of his old apartment that night, leaving behind his working day to flash him a genuine smile, the feeling that came over him was one of admiration.

Andrew tried to smile in return, but the awareness that he wanted something from Stewart sat in his chest. He'd invited him here not for his company, but to ask about Kirsten. He felt his motives were selfish and ulterior.

'How are you?' he asked as he clicked the lid from two bottles of beer. They drank together; that was how they shared their time. He couldn't remember an occasion when they were together and not drinking something. He wasn't sure why two men always needed something to hold on to whenever they were alone together.

'Good, mate. We're busy at work right now. There's a big building going up in the city and we're behind schedule on it. I keep finding myself in boardrooms accounting for the delays.' He took a sip of his beer. 'We could build it faster, but not if they want it to still be standing ten years from now.' He shrugged. 'How about you? I thought you would have been back in Berlin by now.' Stewart was standing near the window. If you stood at the very corner of the room, you could catch a glimpse of Rushcutters Bay, a small triangle bordered by trees, a cluster of anchored white yachts that bobbed on their moorings like toys.

'No, I need to do a few more things before I go back,' he said. 'I've been taking some photos for an exhibition, actually.' As if that explained his visit. 'How's Louise?' He took another swig of his beer.

'We're good.' All his friends did that now, spoke about themselves in the plural, and it hurt him to hear it, with Dom so far away.

'We're having a baby.'

'Wow, that's great news! When is it due?'

'April—quite soon. I'm starting to get a bit nervous. Sorry I didn't tell you any earlier, mate. It was a bit awkward last time I saw you, with what happened to

Kirsten.' He thought about this, that as Stewart and Louise would be having a baby, he would be in London showing his new work. This was the choice he had made with his life.

He asked Stewart the proper things, all the things he knew that he was supposed to ask, about sex and whether they had chosen names. He said that Stewart's parents must be excited about it. Since about the age of thirty, he had learnt to ask these questions. He had learnt to feign happiness for others, knowing he may never have this for himself. He felt as he spoke that he was pushing the words out between his teeth.

He opened his cupboard doors one at a time to try to find something he could serve for them to eat, something that would make it look as though he had planned this, that Stewart was welcome there. But the only shopping he had done was for the things he needed; he hadn't stocked his cupboards, because he wanted to be able to leave for Berlin as soon as he could.

He found some cashews and they slipped from the packet in a cloud of salt and looked meagre and broken in the bowl. He sat down on the opposite side of the table to Stewart and they were both quiet. He tried to think of something to say, something that would seal off the awkwardness that had awoken between them, but the more he searched for something the further away it seemed to be; striking a topic of conversation between them was now a matter of luck.

'Did you get an invite to Stephen's wedding?' Stewart asked.

Andrew shook his head. 'No. Stephen's getting married, is he?'

'Yes, I think it's in May.' He'd been to university with Stephen and the three of them had been good friends, but he hadn't seen Stephen since he left for Berlin.

'Do you see him much these days? We always used to catch up, the three of us. I miss that.'

'Yeah, less since you went to Berlin. You know, life keeps getting in the way.' Stewart looked down and picked at the label of his beer. 'Oh yeah, did you hear about the coronial inquiry?'

For a moment, Andrew thought he'd misheard. He felt a pain in his stomach, as though he'd swallowed a nail.

'Sorry?'

'About Kirsten. They're holding a coronial inquiry into her disappearance. It starts next Monday. Louise heard about it from Kirsten's mother—she spoke to her at the funeral. I thought you might have heard about it too.'

'A coronial inquiry? I didn't realise it was . . . God,' he said.

'Yeah—I mean, I think there was a lot about what happened that has been left unexplained.'

When Stewart left, he realised that if he wanted to go to the coronial inquiry, he would have to postpone his flight again. He'd only postponed it by a week and now he was due to fly out again in a few days. He needed to get back to Dom, but he also needed to know what had happened to Kirsten.

Out over the trees through the windows, bats rose in black shapes that tumbled in the air like black rags caught in the wind and he longed to feel Dom's body against his.

18

On Monday, the morning the coronial inquiry began, he woke early. All he had in his apartment to sleep under was the duvet he'd taken from his mother's house and he woke the next morning too warm and wet with sweat. He rubbed one foot over the other in a nervous gesture and pressed his face into the pillow, willing himself back to sleep, but consciousness had already slipped open inside him.

The things he would hear that day about Kirsten would be difficult; in his life he had always shied away from the details of death. He felt already too accustomed to it, that his life had been defined by it and he had now earned his right to live without hearing any more about it.

He ate his breakfast quickly, chewing his toast and swallowing his coffee without feeling the food was making him full. In the taxi on the way to the coroner's court, he beat his fist to his chest, feeling the food congested there, fighting its way down. That morning he had written the address of the court on a slip of paper, but he had left it on the kitchen bench, forgetting to take it with him when he left the apartment. The taxi driver drove down Glebe Point Road and Bridge Road, but couldn't find the court, and he felt impatience rise in him, thinking he might be missing something essential about Kirsten as he sat there in the back of the car, with motion sickness passing through him.

Eventually they found the building on Parramatta Road, but it was a strange place for a court, with the buzz of traffic outside, passing this solemn place indifferently. He shuffled across the back seat of the cab, paid the driver and stood on his wobbly legs.

Inside the foyer was busy but silent, like a place of worship; people hurried, gathered and waited without speaking. He moved towards a seat outside the courtroom. It had a very straight back, like a church pew.

In his jeans and the blue Adidas sneakers he'd bought in Berlin he felt underdressed. He only had one mode of dressing now: casually, in clothes designed for comfort and ease of movement. He'd long since given up wearing suits. But sitting where he was, he wished he'd dressed more formally and he tucked his feet under his chair, hoping no-one would notice his colourful shoes.

Shortly before ten, the other people in the foyer stood and moved into the courtroom, moving as though responding to a silent bell. He followed them in and found a seat, squeezing along a full row, knees shifting sideways to allow him to pass. The room stood when the magistrate entered, but he found himself still seated, looking at the people around him, mystified by these orchestrated movements. Later he learnt the etiquette, to stand each time the magistrate entered and left the room, and he enjoyed the performance of it; it seemed comical to him, all this standing and sitting and standing again, though no-one else seemed to see the humour in it. In between rows the carpet was worn, in some places down as far as the weaving that held it together and, behind him, the creak of a loose floorboard registered each time a person left the room.

The first person to give evidence that Monday morning was the doctor who had prepared a medical report based on the medication Kirsten had been prescribed. He was talking about benzodiazepines, referring to the empty bottle of pills found in Kirsten's car.

'Assuming the deceased took the whole bottle of tablets, would it have been a lethal dose?' counsel assisting asked. He was a tall man who favoured one leg, with a hand held to his lower back, as though seeking out the source of a pain. During the course of the hearing, the man's back became a familiar sight, the gowns hung from his body in vertical pleats. He shifted his weight from one side to the other, like a horse.

'In my opinion, it's unlikely to have been lethal for someone who took drugs regularly and there's evidence the deceased did so.'

'Could the drug have contributed to her death?'

'It may have done, yes. It's difficult to say without an autopsy.'

Andrew looked down for a moment, feeling the floor move beneath him, and he thought about standing up and leaving. To most people this sort of information was fascinating, but to him it was disturbing and grotesque, that everybody in the room was speaking so plainly about death. He looked around the room for someone to make eye contact with, to share his disbelief, but nobody met his gaze.

Everything that happened in the courtroom seemed to follow a script. There was a strange, rehearsed quality to people's words and expressions, as though what he was watching here was a re-enactment of something that had happened before. He felt angry that they were speaking in such blunt terms about this woman he had known and loved. He forced himself to stay and listen, though there were moments when the witness spoke of possibilities that were macabre and he sat through these details with his eyes closed, the fluorescent lights leaving white streaks on the inside of his lids.

That afternoon, a tall man with arms that moved beside him like oars took a seat in the witness stand and gave his occupation as a cattle farmer. He had been eating lunch that day with his family at the picnic area beside Lake George.

'The lake had been empty for years, but with all the rain recently it was full for the first time since the kids were born. We'd seen it on the news; they weren't sure how long it would stay that way and we, my wife and I—' he glanced towards someone in the courtroom and the people sitting around him turned to look that way '—thought we'd take the kids to see it on the way to Canberra. You never know, with that lake, when it will be full again.' Something stirred in Andrew; he was moved by the effort this man was going to in order to make himself understood. 'We packed a picnic, though it wasn't really the right weather for it. The car was parked there, right by the water. It was the only one parked that close to the lake's edge. I didn't even know whether there was anyone in it. I looked at it, I remember, and wondered if it had been abandoned. I even wondered whether it had been stolen. I mean, it looked brand new.' He was speaking towards his hands. 'We were sitting at one of the picnic tables they have there. It was a cold day.' He looked up. 'My daughter was wearing fingerless gloves.' He smiled and there were gaps between his teeth.

'Did you see the deceased step out of the car?'

The man shook his head. His head was large and the movement of it looked sorrowful.

'No, I didn't. I saw a person duck beneath the fence, but I didn't—I mean, I thought she must be going down there to the water's edge, but when I looked up again, I couldn't see her. I assumed she'd come back to the car without me seeing.'

'So you didn't see her again?'

'No. As we left I checked the car and she wasn't there. I looked out over the lake and I couldn't see anyone. I mean, part of me thought she must've walked too far out by that stage, so that I couldn't see her. The air was misty.'

'And what happened next?'

'I said to my wife I thought I should take a look, you know, just in case. So I went down to the water's edge and stepped through the fence.'

As the man sat in the witness box, Andrew tried to imagine what he would look like hurrying. He was so large that he probably wouldn't be capable of moving very quickly; he had the body of a broad-chested football player whose strength was not in his speed, but in his weight and momentum. 'It was very muddy ground there and I wasn't wearing the right shoes, but when I got to the water's edge, I still couldn't see her. That's when I knew something wasn't right. I mean, she'd just disappeared.'

At the back of the courtroom and to his left, a fluorescent light flickered as he tried to concentrate on what the man was saying. The words he spoke seemed somehow crucial.

•

By the morning of the second day, he understood that the big-boned woman sitting in the front row was Kirsten's mother. She assumed the same position as the previous day. Her shape from behind was solemn, a broad back, her head hanging down. There was a grace to her stillness and the way she sat with her shoulders pulled back, her head tucked into her chest, reminded him of a water bird. She hadn't flinched at all when the doctor spoke of how Kirsten might have died. She hadn't acted the way he assumed a grieving parent would; she didn't leave the room or avert her gaze. She didn't hide her face in her hands; there were no tears shed.

●

When they were together, Kirsten used to see her mother often, though she rarely went home. They met for coffee or lunch and afterwards Kirsten would tell him about it.

'I met Mum today.' Her eyes would be flashing something at him, some signal he never understood. Even though their relationship was volatile, he had the impression that she shared things with her mother, things that she wasn't prepared to tell anyone else, even him. Her mother also gave her money, sometimes a few hundred dollars, and for a few days they would feel rich and spend the money on wine and French cheese. He used to see Kirsten counting it, placing the notes in piles and squaring off the corners. There was always a look of concentration on her face as she performed the task, about the way she counted the money and looked at it as though it bore some significance other than its monetary value.

In spite of the amount of time he'd spent with Kirsten, the only occasion he'd met Kirsten's mother and stepfather together was for a dinner to mark her twenty-first birthday. They went out to an Italian restaurant with Kirsten's mother and stepfather, crossing the bridge to Mosman. Beside him at the table, Kirsten kept shifting in her chair, a small movement that made the chair creak beneath her—it strained as though about to break. Their dinner was strangely quiet, the conversation intermittent; there was a politeness and formality to their words, as though they were being spoken across a great distance, and they seemed unclear about the details of each other's lives. There was a moment when Kirsten's stepfather had to be reminded of what she was studying at university. The silences spread open between them, pockets of air that held an unspoken sadness.

After one of those silences, as he'd spun the last piece of spaghetti around his fork, her stepfather said suddenly, 'Did Peter call today?' There was something in his eyes, something cold and definite like glass that made Andrew think that her stepfather already knew what the answer to his question would be. That might have been the first time he understood that parents have this power over their children, one which it must be tempting to misuse.

In response to those words Kirsten had pulled her arms into her body, like a person caught in an act of theft. She shook her head in a small, almost imperceptible movement.

When the waiter had brought out her birthday cake that night, nobody sang 'Happy Birthday'. Kirsten stared out from behind the glow of the orange flames and Andrew kept having to clear his throat.

Later, on their way back across the bridge to their apartment, she told him as she looked out of the window of the train that Peter was her father's name and that she hadn't seen him in over five years. She rested her head on his shoulder as she spoke.

•

In court on the third morning, Kirsten's mother gave evidence, sitting in the witness stand with her knees pressed together. Her voice was soft and difficult to hear, diffuse with air.

'Could you state your name and occupation for the record?'

'Renee Rothwell. I'm a chartered accountant. Retired.'

'And what was your relationship to the deceased?'

'Her mother.' Her gaze drifted towards him, but her eyes never quite settled on his. Had she recognised him? He must have changed a great deal in the years that had elapsed. He was aware that he no longer looked like a young man; he had silver flecks through his hair, lines around his eyes.

'What was your daughter's occupation, Mrs Rothwell?'

'She was unemployed at the time of the . . . the accident. She went back to university. She had been employed by my husband for a short while, but it didn't work out. Before that, she worked for a barrister as his personal assistant.'

'What did she do for your husband?'

'She worked in the office, answering phones. Administration. Some accounts as well, I think.' She looked beyond the people in the courtroom to the back wall.

'And she was studying?'

'She went back to finish her degree in fine arts. She'd started it straight out of school, but never finished.' Renee looked down. 'Kirsten could draw,' she said, and there was a flash of pride on her face, a brief flicker, like the shine off a coin. Her eyes met his again for another brief moment and then glanced off somewhere behind him.

Spoken in this room full of strangers, among people who would not know what those words meant, they sounded thin; they didn't capture what Kirsten was capable of doing with her hands. Oh, how she could draw! She sat down at the desk in their spare room and the world was lost to her. While she was drawing, he didn't exist. She would copy something—usually a painting from a book—and when he saw her sitting there, inside her fortress of concentration, he envied how easy it was for her to withdraw. While they lived together, she had copied all of the paintings from a book on Vermeer she picked up second-hand at the Glebe markets. She captured the same light of his paintings, a light that rained down like water. She could do it just with the shading of her pencil. Her drawings were precise, somehow more exact than the originals.

'She was at the National Art School last year. I helped her financially, so she could go back and study, but I was told she dropped out. I hadn't known that.'

This was how Kirsten's life was accounted for in the end, with these few things that she had attempted but at which she had never quite succeeded. If his own life were summarised at the end, and if he took away photography and Dom, it might look as empty and insignificant as Kirsten's.

•

The faces he saw each day in the courtroom became familiar and he watched some of the journalists filing into court together and shuffling out again in the afternoon, exchanging comments about the proceedings. They were all waiting for that moment, for the critical revelation, the one fact that would unravel the mystery of Kirsten's death, as though there were a single explanation, one way to understand what she had done that day.

Outside the courtroom, Kirsten's mother spoke to no-one. At lunchtime, she sat on the wooden bench outside the court room and ate a sandwich, taking very small bites. A journalist approached her during an adjournment and Andrew watched as she held her small palm up to him before he drew too close. He watched her from the foyer of the court, standing with his back to the wall, waiting for the right opportunity to speak to her, but in truth he was frightened of what her reaction to him might be.

Would she blame him? Accuse him? There were moments in a person's life, and once they had happened, one could not always recover from them. He felt that way about his father's death: he was not the same person after it as he had been before it. Perhaps Renee Rothwell would accuse him of being that to Kirsten, of somehow breaking her. He feared she would tell him that all of this, Kirsten's decline, had somehow started with him.

He watched her intently. During the proceedings, Kirsten's mother spoke to no-one except occasionally to counsel assisting the inquiry, when he swivelled around in his chair to ask a question during the course of the hearing, and even then her answers were restricted to one or two words.

Andrew spent more time observing her than watching what was happening in the hearing. He observed how still she sat; she might have been a marble bust. There was something about the way she sat unmoving that suggested reluctance and made him think she was there against her will.

•

The police officer who'd been responsible for investigating the death gave evidence on the fourth day of the hearing. It was late in the morning and he sounded weary, the words he spoke dredged up from a dark and difficult place. Kirsten drove to Canberra from Sydney that morning in a car she had borrowed from her stepfather. It had been purchased by her stepfather's company three months before Kirsten's disappearance. Kirsten had stopped at Goulburn.

'Was there any reason that you're aware of for her making that stop?' counsel assisting asked.

The police officer shifted in his chair and his eyes flicked briefly towards her mother.

'She bought fifteen dollars' worth of petrol and a loaf of bread.'

'Sorry, did you say a loaf of bread?'

'Yes. She went back to buy it after she'd paid for the petrol. I reviewed the CCTV footage.'

Bread, Andrew thought, clutching at this detail, holding it to his chest, trying to locate the significance it held within it. A person who buys bread surely intends to live. He wanted to stand up and say, *There, you see, she wanted to eat! She wanted to live!*

He imagined her in the grainy black-and-white footage, walking in and out of the shop alone. There must have been footage of him like that everywhere, doing everyday things that, when you looked back at them, appeared strange and inexplicable to others. But when you died the way Kirsten did, this was what happened: people raked through the details of your life and tried to make sense of it.

In Canberra, Kirsten went to Ainslie, where she'd driven up and down the same street—Campbell Street—a number of times. It had been reported to police as suspicious. The police officer said he wasn't sure if there was any significance to that street and it was the only time Kirsten's mother moved. She stood from her chair, rising above the seated bodies towards counsel assisting. She whispered something into his ear and the barrister tilted his head towards her. It looked intimate, even solicitous.

When she sat down again, counsel assisting stood and said, 'Your Honour, I'm informed by the deceased's mother that Campbell Street in Ainslie is where the deceased's sister resides, at number fifty-two.'

Kirsten had spoken of her sister to him, although they'd never met. The tone of Kirsten's voice whenever she'd uttered Lydia's name was bright and warm, like someone standing in darkness and speaking of light.

Counsel assisting then asked about the search for her body.

'We spent two days there conducting a full-scale search. We flew in divers from the search and rescue squad in Sydney,' the police officer said, his voice higher, tighter, as though anticipating criticism. He looked to the magistrate and back to the barrister. 'We didn't have the manpower to search the whole lake,' he conceded.

'It's twenty-five kilometres long and ten wide, and was fuller than it's been in years. It holds hundreds of millions of litres of water.'

•

That afternoon at three, counsel assisting stood and declared there was no more evidence. Somehow, just like that, in a single sentence and a sweeping gesture of this barrister's hand, the hearing was over.

The magistrate stood abruptly and left the room, and everybody else stood and lingered, as if waiting for a more emphatic conclusion. Not Kirsten's mother though. She stood and moved straight to the door with her head down, like a criminal absolved of a crime. Andrew hurried out behind her, pushing the weight of the heavy courtroom door away from him with both his hands.

'Mrs Rothwell?' he called, but she didn't seem to hear him. 'Excuse me?'

She was almost at the front door when she turned around to face him. Outside, the traffic on Parramatta Road sped past, the sound reaching him through the door in snippets, like a radio station not quite tuned to a signal. He felt a nerve next to his eye twinge.

'I'm not sure if you remember me,' he said, wishing as he spoke the words that he could explain it to her more delicately, that he wasn't always racing towards a resolution. 'I used to—I mean, Kirsten used to be my girlfriend.' He ran his fingers through his hair. He wasn't sure what Kirsten had told her mother about them.

Kirsten's mother tilted her head, as though with this movement, she was trying to recall a younger version of him. She was wearing a small gold cross on her necklace that hung over the sunken space at the base of her neck where her collarbones met. She had a strong jawline and the wrinkles around her mouth were ambiguous, he couldn't be sure whether they had been formed from laughing or pursing. As he kept talking, he had the sensation of swimming in dark water, aware that he couldn't see the bottom and there might be something lurking not far beneath him.

'I'm sorry. Someone else—a mutual friend—told me about the inquiry and I wanted to know more about it. I suppose this must be quite strange for you?' He knew as he said it that the word *strange* wasn't quite enough, that it did not carry the heft it needed, because what they were discussing was the death of this woman's daughter.

When she spoke, her eyes were fixed on his chest. 'I see. Well. I think I remember you. I'm glad you introduced yourself,' she said. But glad was not how she appeared. Her face was heavy and hard, set like a theatre mask. She took a step backwards and reached for the door. 'It's nice to know you still cared about Kirsten.' She said this with an air of finality.

He didn't want her to go. His instinct was to reach for the door and press it closed, to prevent her from leaving. 'I wondered whether you'd be willing to talk to me about her. You see, we lost touch and . . .' He saw her frown. He licked his lips and continued. 'I wondered if you could tell me a little more about what happened to her. I've been living overseas for the past few years. I'd like to know more.'

Mrs Rothwell straightened and tightened her grip on her handbag. They stepped away from the door to allow other people to leave. He noticed the way she moved her hands, how she reached for the front door and held her hand now, to her bag, touching things so lightly she looked reluctant to make contact. Her hands might have been covered in gloves.

'Well, I'm sorry. As I'm sure you can understand, the last few days have been quite difficult. I need some time. What if I call you?' She looked past him. She was speaking in a breathy voice that sounded as though it should have been coming from another person's mouth, someone younger and less sure of themselves.

'I'll give you my number,' he said. 'I'd appreciate it if you called me, when you feel ready.' He didn't actually want to leave it up to her, but what choice did he have?

He handed her a piece of paper with his phone number on it and watched the door swing shut. Behind him the foyer had emptied.

19

That evening, he emailed the images to the gallery in London as thumbnails, including the photos of Phoebe. He hadn't heard anything from Pippa and it had been more than a week. He hesitated before he pressed send, wondering if he should call Pippa just to make sure she had no objection, but part of him didn't want to give her the opportunity to say no.

The gallery called late that night, while he was asleep.

'It's Marten Smythe here,' a clipped voice said when he answered the phone.

'Sorry?' He sat up in bed, his thoughts rushing back towards consciousness.

'Marten Smythe, London Six,' the voice said.

'Oh yes. I'm in Australia—it's late here. Could you

give me a few moments?'

'Oh, you're back in Australia, are you? Of course, take your time.'

He walked to the kitchen with the phone and filled the upturned glass on the sink with water. Through the kitchen window he saw the moon glowing through a thin layer of cloud as though behind silk, light bleeding out around it. He picked up the phone again.

'I'm sorry,' he said, still feeling foggy from sleep.

'That's quite all right. I was just calling to talk about your photos.'

He worried suddenly that Marten was calling to say the images weren't what he wanted. That he was calling off the exhibition and everything Andrew had been working towards would be for nothing.

Instead, Marten said, 'We're really excited about this work. We'd like to have the prints ready as soon as we can. Could you send the high-resolution images over on a USB stick? By courier, if you could.'

It took him a moment to readjust himself to this development and there was a sudden jerk of feeling, a leap from one place to another.

'Oh right, wow. Yes, of course.'

'Splendid. Also, the girl with the face . . .' *The girl with the face.* He wanted to tell this man that her name was Phoebe and that she was a lovely, complicated girl. That she was more than her face. Marten continued, 'It's almost excruciating to look at, the level of detail, it almost makes me want to look away. I have a feeling about it. It's unique. I think it will sell well. The photograph of the young boy with his eyes closed, too. I think you called it *Smiling Alone*. Very striking. Really, in my opinion this is your most sophisticated body of work yet.'

He didn't like to be reminded of the fact that art was a business and that, like any other business, in the end it turned on money. These conversations with gallery owners and curators stripped him of his naive belief that art was about art. And now he was acutely aware of how he was involving Phoebe in this fickle world of his. He thought of the images of Phoebe and started to worry that somehow they were too honest. They took advantage of her openness and maybe they were too exposing to be shown. Maybe if he exhibited those images, he would be putting on display a personal transaction that had taken place between him and Phoebe; an interaction that was essentially private and should not be shown to the world.

In the morning, he put the exhibition photographs on a USB stick but saved the photographs of Phoebe on a separate stick. He sent the first lot of photos, but the photographs of Phoebe he kept. He put them in a drawer in his apartment. He would take a few more days to think it over.

•

The next day he went back to his mother's house to collect some clothes he'd left there. It was just after one in the afternoon and he had chosen a time when he assumed his mother would be at work and he could slip in and out without seeing her. He didn't want to risk her trying to talk to him again about his father. He had gone too long without speaking about it and now his only natural response to it was silence.

But his mother walked in from a shift at the hospital in her black slacks and white blouse just as he was about to leave.

Since she'd brought up the matter of his father's death, they hadn't spoken properly. When he had seen her, the words that passed between them were reduced to what was necessary, they were quick and brief and spoken with no feeling.

She made herself a cup of tea and sat down at the kitchen table. He sat down opposite her.

'I thought you were supposed to be heading back last weekend?' his mother said, gently.

'I was,' he said. He wasn't sure how much he wanted to share with his mother now. He sighed, trying to keep his lingering anger hidden from her. 'But there was a coronial inquiry into Kirsten's death. It finished on Wednesday. I stayed for that.'

His mother looked up, eager for whatever words he was prepared to share with her. She might have accepted anything from him just then, even an insult.

'She took some pills before she drowned.' He heard the hardness in his voice, and the callousness in those words as he spoke them was aimed at her.

He watched the words impact her.

'Oh, Andrew. What happened?'

'I still don't know exactly. The coroner hasn't handed down her findings.'

'God, that's terrible,' she said. She went quiet, moving to the kitchen without saying anything more. He watched her closely in order to observe the effect his words had had on her.

Darkness passed across her face. 'She was always so . . .' His mother hesitated. 'She always seemed so troubled.' She blew on her tea and continued before he could answer her. 'I could always see that about her— that she was too fragile for the world. Everything always seemed to affect her very deeply.' His mother's words were faint. She looked out into the yard without saying any more, but he could tell that Kirsten was still lodged in her thoughts. There was something about Kirsten that always seemed to linger, a mystery, and he understood by looking at his mother now that he wasn't the only one who had sensed it.

●

That night, he had just stepped out of the shower when his telephone rang.

'Hello?'

'It's Renee Rothwell.'

'Oh, hello,' he said, realising abruptly he was speaking with Kirsten's mother.

'My husband and I would like to invite you to have morning tea with us. Tomorrow if that would suit you?'

Morning tea sounded very formal.

'Okay, that suits me.' He spoke the words too quickly and tried to settle his own feeling of urgency.

'Why don't we say eleven, then?'

'Great.'

She gave him her address and directions from the train station at Gordon. He had the feeling of having been summoned and that night, he waited and paced and ate and slept like someone waiting to receive bad news.

20

On the way to Renee's house on the train, he realised that he should have brought something with him. Something to offer them. If he had thought about it earlier, he could have bought something from the sourdough bakery near his apartment. He thought of the pastel-coloured macarons in the glass cabinet, but they were too bright, playful. Or maybe he should have brought flowers, but he wasn't sure how he would have decided on the right colour.

The metal struts slid across the window beside him as he passed over the Harbour Bridge. The harbour was a broken blue, the uninviting darkness of very deep water.

Exiting the station at Gordon, he saw a small bakery. Inside it was warm and smelt of yeast and sultanas. The bread was stacked on the shelves, loaves and loaves of it, the dimensions exact, pushed from the same mould, white, fluffy and lacking in nourishment.

He missed the German bread he'd grown used to in Berlin, heavy and substantial. He bought a fruit loaf that felt soft when he picked it up and light as he carried it from the shop. Further down the street, he slowed down. He was going to speak to these people about their dead daughter and what he had to offer them was a flimsy loaf of bread. He stopped and packed it into his backpack so it would be hidden.

The noise from the highway receded behind the lines of houses and he found himself on a quiet street. The wind jostled the trees around him, hostile. A crow flew past, its cry desolate and forlorn, three long pleas with no variation in tone.

There was nothing remarkable or grand about these houses. They were the sorts of red-brick dwellings that people lived in everywhere, but here, in these suburbs, they were spacious and well cared for—they said something about the wealth of the people who lived in them. They weren't like the houses in Leichhardt that had been added to and built on and threatened to burst from their lawns. They were houses that remained confined to the seams that contained them. In these driveways were new cars of moderate tones, the types of cars that slipped through the world and attracted no dirt. In the gardens were hedges and topiary plants and in their windows, the curtains were drawn. The houses he passed were utterly still; they were houses from which all the children had gone.

When he reached Kirsten's old house, there was a poinciana tree in the front lawn that had shed its leaves and its trunk was as scaly and smooth as a reptile. The branches were bare and, against the red bricks behind it, the frame looked ghostly. It stood in the yard obstructing the front lawn and it took him a moment to notice the path around it.

'Good morning,' Renee said when she opened the door.

The first thing he noticed was that she was wearing a knee-length navy skirt and stockings and he wondered what type of person dressed so formally on a Saturday in their own home. He walked in behind her and down a hall lined with photographs hung along the picture rail. It was as though these photographs constituted proof of what these people had accomplished with their lives, documentary evidence of a useful and productive existence. They were photos that asked no questions.

There was a photograph of a girl with dark hair, a toddler, sitting in the haphazard way of a child who hasn't learnt to walk and is yet to find her centre of gravity. She was sitting on the edge of a roundabout with her feet dragging in the gravel. The girl's nose scrunched up tightly and her hair was thin and wispy; there was barely enough to be pulled together in a ponytail. She was wearing pink and the smile on her face was one that had never known sadness.

The young girl might have been Kirsten, it looked like her, but it might also have been her sister, who he had never met. He lingered there, but ahead of him Renee had disappeared into a room so he followed her. He didn't ask about the picture; it felt somehow impolite to ask about a dead woman in a photograph.

Inside, the furnishings were new. He had assumed that people like this, older people whose children had left home and whose careers would soon be ending, would hold on to the things they had collected over the years, that their furniture would accumulate in their house as they aged. But it was new and there was too much of it. It was placed too closely together and everywhere it looked to be in the way.

For a moment, he was distracted by the clutter and didn't see Kirsten's stepfather standing there. He was behind the couch so that Andrew could only see him from above the waist, like a puppet on stage.

'Saul,' he said, holding out his hand for Andrew to shake.

His beard had turned completely white since they'd last met, but if he had any recollection of Andrew he didn't show it as he leant forward over the lounge and shook his hand. His hands were large and forceful like a boxer's. He wondered whether Renee had explained to her husband exactly who he was and why he was here.

On the coffee table Italian biscuits were arranged on a white plate, the china so fine the light passed through it. They were delicate biscuits laid out like ornaments. Some of them were shaped like horseshoes, covered with flaked almonds, others were pistachio green. He thought of the fruit loaf in the bag that he put at his feet when he sat down, glad now it remained hidden and that he wouldn't have to embarrass himself by offering it to Renee.

'Can I offer you some tea or coffee?' she asked.

'I'd love a tea,' he said.

She nodded and left for the kitchen and her husband stayed standing in the room. His features looked oversized, his nose and ears too large for his face; ageing had made his skin retreat from his features. His eyes were glassy, like the stuffed head of an animal on a wall. Those creatures had the same look about them as Kirsten's stepfather, of not quite believing where they had found themselves.

'What is it you do with yourself?'

'I'm a photographer.'

'Oh yeah? I suppose you work for a newspaper or a magazine?'

'Well, no.' He still found it hard to explain his occupation to other people. 'My photographs are more like portraits.'

'I see. I'm a salesperson myself. I own an office supply business.' He coughed on the back of his hand.

Renee walked in with a tray on which was a delicate teapot the colour of crushed bones. She put it down on the table in front of her, making the movement awkwardly, without bending her knees.

She poured tea then sat on the lounge opposite him, crossing one leg over the other and tugging her skirt over her knees with her fingers. 'Are you working at the moment?' she asked.

'I, well, I'm preparing for an exhibition that's opening next month.' A crease of anxiety unfolded inside him as he thought of the photographs of Phoebe he still hadn't sent to the gallery. What he was doing would threaten the professional reputation it had taken him years to build.

Renee sat in the corner of the lounge, holding one hand inside the other as though she'd been taught somewhere the proper way of sitting and had practised the pose until it became her habit.

'Oh, I see,' she said softly, fiddling with the cross on her necklace.

Saul stayed standing with the cup in his hand. He couldn't keep his hand still and the teacup rattled on its saucer.

'You know, we saw Kirsten quite regularly,' he said loudly, over the clatter of his teacup. Renee pushed the sleeves of her cardigan up. 'She came here to visit. She still had her own room here.' He looked out the window as he spoke.

Andrew reached for a biscuit, but realised that neither Renee nor her husband had taken one. His hand hovered as he wondered whether they were only there for display. Renee nodded her head in a very slight movement that made it look as though she didn't want to be seen. He took a horseshoe-shaped biscuit and held it in his hand, waiting for someone else to take one too. The biscuit grew sticky in his palm as he waited.

'She asked to borrow the car for the day, you know?' Renee's husband started again. 'She came into the office the week before to ask me. She told me she wanted to go to Canberra to see an exhibition. What was it again, Renee?' He was a man who always spoke with a frown, a man for whom the world seemed to be a very confusing place.

'She was going to visit the National Gallery,' Renee said, looking down.

'And when I found out what she'd done, I just—' He stopped and looked into his tea. He spoke as though Kirsten's death had offended rather than upset him. 'How could I have known what she intended to do?' His cheeks were sharply sunken, forming two divots in his skin.

Saul cleared his throat and looked at Renee, and Andrew understood that by coming here as a person from Kirsten's past, he had invited this. Somehow Saul thought that, if he could explain himself to Andrew, explain how he thought he might have contributed to Kirsten's fate, he would be forgiven, as though Andrew, being someone who had once loved her, had that power.

He was expecting the biscuit to snap in his mouth when he bit into it, but it was soft and crumbly and broke apart. He cupped his hand to his mouth to stop the pieces from falling to the floor.

'Did she . . .' he started to say. 'I mean, had she . . . Was she all right before?' He couldn't say the word *accident*, the word everyone else kept using to describe what had happened to Kirsten, though it hardly seemed to have been accidental. It seemed to be thought out, planned and deliberate. If nothing else, that much was clear.

'She seemed happy enough, didn't she, Renee? Last time we saw her, anyway.'

'Yes,' Renee said, looking up, but there was a heaviness to her features, the way a person looks when they are speaking of one thing but thinking of another.

'Well, Andrew,' Saul said, taking the last sip of his tea. Andrew thought he was being dismissed, so he stood as well, but the other man continued, 'I'm going out to work in the garden. Saturdays are the only chance I get. I'll leave you two here to talk.'

He sat down again and felt relief as Saul left. Renee was still fiddling with the cross at her neck, as though some memory were attached to it. He was quiet and she was quiet and then they both spoke at the same time.

'You go,' he said.

'I'm glad you came. I mean, when I saw you that day at court, it was very sudden.'

He supposed to her it seemed sudden, although to him it wasn't that way; he'd been thinking about what to say to her for days.

'I heard you say at the hearing that Kirsten had gone back to art school?' he said.

'Yes,' she replied. 'She went back to the National Art School. I think she wanted to try to pick up where she left off from her old degree. But it had been too many years.' She pressed her knees against her hands. 'She was out of practice.'

'She was . . .' He didn't know how to capture what he thought in words. 'Her drawings were wonderful. It always upset me that she left university.'

'Yes, they were, weren't they?' she said gently and he wondered if Renee had ever tried to dissuade her from leaving.

'Do you know if there was someone else in Kirsten's life?' The words skittered from his mouth and her lips twisted in response to his question.

'It's so hard to say with Kirsten. She was a bit . . . I don't know. In the end, she didn't always tell me everything.'

He wondered, then, if they'd spoken about him, if Kirsten had told her mother how for years they'd lived apart and slept together. Maybe he should tell this woman that he had wanted to help Kirsten, but he just didn't have what it took to do that for another person.

Then her tone changed, it turned warmer. 'She worked for a few years for a barrister as his personal assistant.' She articulated the last two words carefully. 'She did enjoy that in the beginning.' She rearranged her hands on her lap. 'He was quite prominent and I think the work made her feel important.'

'Did you see her?' he asked. 'Before it happened?'

She stiffened and pressed her knees together. 'I hadn't seen her properly for a few weeks. She picked up the car from Saul at work. She seemed busy. I thought that was a good thing.' Renee looked up and her eyes narrowed. 'We really tried. I mean, my husband gave her a job after she'd stopped working for the barrister. Even though she'd said some things to me about Saul that were hurtful.' She looked into her lap.

He could see Renee was angry at Kirsten for dying the way she had. She took Kirsten's death as an insult, a personal accusation. He looked at the biscuits on the coffee table, wondering if it would be rude of him to take another one. He wasn't sure why he felt so hungry suddenly; there was an ache in his teeth for something sweet.

A dark look passed over her face. 'The barrister she worked for was married,' she said, filling her words with air, as though she was blowing them towards him. There was an edge in her gaze almost of menace. He shifted and underneath him the leather couch protested.

'Had *you* seen Kirsten recently?' she asked, looking across at him, her gaze steely. She had the look about her of someone who already knows. He thought for a moment that answering her question might be like handing her something he would never get back again.

He conceded that he had not and he knew what she was doing. With her words, she was questioning his right to be there at all. He felt a sudden urge to make a confession. He thought that must be what she wanted from him.

'I know that I didn't handle things with Kirsten the way I should have,' he found himself saying. He felt distant from his words. 'But we were both young.'

From the look on her face he could tell this was not what she had wanted to hear.

On the way out of the house he saw through a window, Saul on his knees in the garden. He wore a white terry-towelling hat and was tilling the soil with a small gardening fork, snail bait sprinkled over the garden bed. The pellets were an unnatural green against the soil.

'Good-bye,' Andrew said to Renee, turning back towards her as he left.

'Thank you for coming,' she said. 'God bless.'

Looking back towards her, the way she stood in the doorway of her own home, formally dressed with her arms folded across her body, he had the impression of someone being slowly smothered, of drowning on air.

21

On Monday afternoon he walked through Darlinghurst towards the National Art School where Kirsten had gone back to study. The only clouds in the sky were long webbed strands, like spidery veins. Though it was late in the day, the heat ebbed and moved across the bitumen in swirls. The sandstone walls surrounding the college were fat and tall, the large wooden gates painted green and held together by cast iron.

The buildings inside were oddly shaped sandstone blocks. One fat, round building in the middle of the grounds looked like a watch house. The buildings he passed obscured the path behind him and he turned back, feeling disorientated, as though navigating his way through a labyrinth.

Students stood talking in small huddles. One young man wore a waistcoat and the woman he was talking to wore a long, pleated skirt that almost brushed the ground. They stood together with their arms folded looking poised, like people waiting to have their photographs taken. He remembered this from art school: the feeling that people were looking at him as though they didn't particularly like him. What the years had taught him since was that mostly what other people felt about him wasn't even as strong as dislike, but was something closer to neutral.

He walked into the building with an open door and it was bigger inside than he expected, the ceilings arched, wooden beams exposed. He might have walked inside the hull of an upturned boat. There were easels set up in the room for a class, but nobody was painting at them. The room smelt of linseed oil and turpentine, hard and metallic. In the centre of the room were stuffed animals on metal spikes. He walked a wide circle around them: a rabbit, a cat and a marsupial he didn't recognise, all with thinning hair. Their eyes glassy and glistening, dead animals that had no other purpose but to be painted. Through a glass door at the back of the building, he could see someone moving about in the small room.

'Hello?' He pushed the door slightly ajar.

'Hi,' the man said, looking up. 'Are you lost?' His eyes were a pale blue, like a husky's. His chin was prominent and he wore his jeans low around his waist.

Andrew stood in the doorway, while the man continued to work. 'Just having a bit of a sticky beak. Screen-printing?' he asked, looking at what the man was working on. The bench was cluttered; a wide brush with coarse black hairs, a pot of black paint and a spray can of fixative.

'Woodblock prints,' the man replied. He cut into a block with a small chisel and a fine shaving curled up, which he brushed away.

Andrew moved around to the opposite side of the table, in order to see the prints the right way up. The shapes were strong and bold, a print of a woman, her face elongated and limbs thick, like a stone sculpture from Easter Island.

'Great shapes,' he said.

'Thanks.'

'Do you work here?'

The man nodded. 'It's handy for my own work,' he said, smiling easily.

Andrew gripped the back of a chair. 'Did you ever come across a student named Kirsten Rothwell?' he asked and the man looked at him for a long moment.

'Yeah, I did.'

'What did you think about her?'

'Not a journalist are you, mate?' the man said, dipping the block of wood into a basin of fluid.

'Nah, a photographer actually. Artistic. My name's Andrew Spruce.' He cleared his throat. He could feel something loose inside it, like the movement in a rattle.

The man looked up, his blue eyes striking Andrew's for the first time. 'Oh yeah, I know your work. The man with the teeth, right?' He looked back down. 'She only studied here for one semester. And she was a bit unusual.'

'Unusual how?'

The man was older than he had initially thought. As Andrew moved closer, he saw the lines in the man's face were deep, like grooves in wood.

'Are you a friend of hers?'

Andrew nodded.

'She just didn't really fit in,' he said. He shrugged. 'I don't know why. Maybe because she was older than the other students. That, and art schools can be difficult places to fit in at the best of times.' The man looked up at him with eyes that betrayed none of his thoughts. 'Don't get me wrong. I thought she had talent. I had her in one of my classes. I mean, you know, there is a lot of talent in a place like this. The thing was, she only ever copied other people's work.'

'She plagiarised?'

'No, she'd see something in a book and draw it exactly as it was, without any interpretation of her own. The drawings were technically good, but that's not enough. I tried to encourage her to find her own subjects, to work out what meant something to her, but she found any criticism quite difficult.'

He wanted to know about Kirsten and yet he was apprehensive, for fear that what he discovered might lead back to him. Everything he heard about her he scanned for implication, for the direction in which it cast out its lines, for which way it pointed.

'Did you hear what happened to her?' he said, aware that the way he was speaking of Kirsten made it sound as though she was a stranger to him, that through this man he was allowing himself some distance from her.

The man wiped his hands on a grey rag and looked up. 'Yeah, people talked about it here, after it happened.'

'What did you think?'

'Well, I don't know. It wasn't exactly clear what she did, but I can't say it entirely surprised me either.' He tipped the basin of fluid into the sink and moved towards the door. The smell of chemicals lingered in the air. 'Sorry, mate, I have to lock this place up now.' He closed the door and looked at him. 'Actually, I think I still have a drawing of hers in my office. I called the contact number on her admission form, but I could never get hold of anyone. I left a message on the machine. I can show it to you if you're interested?'

'I'd love to see it,' he said. 'It's been a long time since I saw any of her work. I mean, I always thought she'd do something with it.' He remembered how her drawings had always produced a feeling with sharp edges, an envy at the fact that Kirsten had produced that work with her own hands.

At the door to his office, the man slipped the key into the lock and pushed his weight against the door. He switched on the fluorescent lights and they fluttered and buzzed with a static charge like neon signs.

'Actually, she's an old girlfriend of mine,' Andrew said, tying himself to her and aware that this information might cast him in a different light.

The man didn't respond. 'Here they are.' He lifted a large cardboard folder from behind his desk and Andrew saw Kirsten's name written across the front. He recognised her handwriting, an artist's script in which attention is paid to the shape and symmetry of each letter.

He took the first page out and knew it immediately as a copy of Goya's *Saturn Devouring His Son*. It looked to have been drawn in charcoal and the shading was detailed, the strokes soft and filigree, the attention to light and dark exquisite.

Many years ago, he'd seen the original in Madrid, stood in front of it and something had wilted inside him. The whites of the old man's eyes, the fear and madness he felt at the prospect of being usurped by his own child; between his hands an adult's body, the size of a baby, the old man clutching its waist with both hands like a lover. He couldn't help but think that what Saturn was doing in consuming his son was trying to silence him, and maybe all parents had this instinct in relation to their own children. Maybe all parents fear what their children might have to say to them.

It was hard to look at this image now with the knowledge of what had happened to Kirsten and for a brief moment he felt that image, when it rushed off the page and towards him. It couldn't have been very long that he stood there staring at it, but it was long enough for him to have the feeling of returning to the room after having been absent from it, of remembering where he was, looking up and around and taking in air.

The man was checking his emails on his computer, his back to Andrew.

'It's spooky, isn't it? Hard to look at, now. It's a shame she didn't stick at it. Maybe it would have helped.' He was shutting his computer down. 'Sorry, mate, I really have to go.'

'Okay, sure,' Andrew said. 'What will happen to this drawing now?'

The man pulled his office door closed behind them. 'I'll try the number I have once more, but otherwise, I'll have to destroy it.'

Andrew thought of Renee and wondered whether she didn't want to see Kirsten's work, if she wanted to remain ignorant of what it was that had preoccupied her daughter's thoughts as she drew in those months before she died. He thought of Renee's house, her appearance, the level of control she exerted over the things around her.

He walked out of the building and into the courtyard, where a group of students was lingering after a class, bags over their shoulders, adjusting their bodies to the weight and hugging their books to their chests. A young woman held his gaze indifferently. As he walked out onto Forbes Street, he realised he'd been gritting his teeth. A pain grew in his temples, a hot, tight feeling like a cramp.

On Oxford Street, he decided he would do something he had not done in years. He would go into a bar alone and find someone to talk to. He found a pub and sat at the bar and watched women loosely, without any specific interest, in order to remind himself what women who came to bars looked like. He tried not to think of what Dom would think if she saw him here in a place like this.

It was early evening and the women in the bar wore dresses and high heels, standing in lopsided, precarious postures. They looked pinched, their personalities folded up into a neat place inside them, the words they spoke and the clothes they wore might have been traced along dotted lines.

He asked the barman for a drink with vodka. The thought of making conversation occurred to him in a distant sort of way. As he sat there he remembered why he rarely did this. He never enjoyed the conversations that took place in bars, the false note of what people spoke of in bars, of two strangers assessing each other and discussing surface concerns.

A woman with straight blonde hair whom he'd been looking at without any real awareness of where his gaze had fallen moved towards him. She lifted one leg and slid onto the stool beside his. This woman had the look about her of someone who is easy in the world, who could laugh and enjoy herself. He had always been fascinated by people like her, people who were free in all the ways he felt limited.

'You're here alone?' she asked. Her voice had a sultry, broken quality, striking between two notes.

'Yes. I'm staying close by,' he said, gesturing in the direction of his apartment with his arm. Somehow, in the space of three weeks, he'd slipped towards this fate. He had become a man who sat in a bar alone and drank vodka.

'I'm Deb,' she said, and he could smell the alcohol on her breath.

'Andrew.'

'And what do you do?' She swayed slightly on her stool.

'I'm a photographer.' He looked down at the vodka, which was suddenly unappealing.

She inched her hand towards him until their fingers touched. The feeling this gesture provoked in him was of a reptile slipping from a warm rock into a dark pool.

'A photographer?' she said and signalled to the man behind the bar. 'I'm a recruitment consultant. I'll have a martini,' she said to the barman. 'And for you?' He shook his head and held his hand over his drink. 'Come on,' Deb said. 'My shout. Whatever that is,' she said to the barman and pointed at his empty glass.

He sat on his stool and thought how sad it was to have come to this bar for company; that at thirty-seven he found himself here.

'What sort of photos do you take?'

'Mostly portraits,' he said. He looked up. Every surface around him was reflective. He kept his head down so he wouldn't have to watch himself talking to this woman.

'So, head shots and that sort of thing?'

'It depends.'

'On what?'

'On what the subject looks like and how I want the image to look.' He had the feeling when he spoke to her that he was bearing his teeth.

'You know you're not a very easy person to have a conversation with?'

'You're not the first person to tell me that.' There were people who lived inside themselves and those who lived their lives externally and he had already accepted which of the two he was.

'I'm an artistic photographer,' he said, looking into his drink. No matter how many years he'd done it, it didn't get any easier for him to admit this fact to strangers. There was always a tentative feeling about what he did with his life. He remained aware that what he did was something that could easily be taken from him.

'I suppose the people I photograph are unusual in some way,' he said, thinking of the photographs of Phoebe, of her awkwardness and how she was aware of herself in a way that other children her age were not. When he looked at Phoebe he felt he could understand her.

Deb tilted her head at him. 'Unusual?'

'Yes, I suppose that's it.' He took a deep breath. He was a person who had to remind himself to be kind. Being hard on other people and himself was something that came to him too easily. Sometimes he felt he moved through the world with edges as sharp as knives.

She readjusted herself on her stool. The music in the bar sounded suddenly louder.

'It must be wonderful to be able to do that with your life,' she said. Her words were encouraging, but her smile was uncertain. This was the response he drew from people; he knew it too well. His self-consciousness confused them. These were the moments he wished he was someone who could slide through his life and pretend he felt no doubt.

'Yes. Although I've done it for a long time.' His sigh was heavy.

'Why do you keep doing it?' It was a question he had often verged on, but never dared ask of himself. He couldn't afford to. He had invested so much of himself in his work, sometimes he wondered if there would be anything left of him without it.

'There are moments,' he said, unsure how to finish his sentence. Maybe all there were in life were moments, brief occasions when you could look around you and find that the good things in your life had converged. Maybe everyone lived for those moments and in between was just a sort of waiting for things to turn better or to change. Maybe the question of living was how to survive those in-between times.

She gazed at him for a long moment. 'You look sad about something,' she said, but he knew that if you looked at anything for long enough you could eventually see its sadness.

'Maybe I am,' he said defiantly. Sometimes, in the world he lived in, he felt sadness was something that had to be defended. Part of what he did in his work, he thought, was to fight for its rightful place.

'It doesn't sound like you have that much to be sad about.'

How could he explain it to her, that the things that happened to him in his life seemed to cling to him? The same things other people brushed from themselves like lint.

'I don't know. Maybe I've done bad things in my life. Hurt other people.' He looked at her fiercely as he said this, perhaps attempting to flash her some sort of warning.

She looked at him carefully.

This was too much. He wasn't a man who discussed his problems with strangers at a bar. He was a man who rarely discussed them with anyone. He also had no desire to stay sitting there and allow himself to become one. He stood and took his wallet from the back pocket of his jeans, removing a twenty-dollar note and pressing it to the bar.

'Oh, don't go. Come on. Stay. We can talk about something else,' Deb said.

'Sorry,' he said. 'I'm just in a bad frame of mind. Honestly, it would be much better if I left.'

She took hold of his wrist. 'I don't want to go home alone tonight,' she said. He found himself looking at her lips. Her lipstick formed a line around the edges of her mouth. He looked away and tried to muster something, that instinct that had once been so familiar to him, the desire to be inside someone, the urge to move beyond himself.

'It's just . . . I love someone,' he said and she released her grip on his wrist.

He left the bar. Outside it was windy and he put his hands into the pockets of his jacket and started walking towards Darlinghurst. Along Riley, just past Foveaux Street, he stopped on a corner outside a terrace house painted dark green, the colour of camouflage, as though attempting to hide in plain view. The windows were tinted, reflecting the streetlights, and there was the glow of a red lamp next to the door. Why was it that he never saw people entering these types of places?

Everything about the building suggested discretion, it said you could walk in there and out again without there being any trace of your visit. The traffic lights changed twice as he stood there looking at the door and the traffic swelled past him. Someone yelled as a car passed.

He kept walking. On Oxford Street, the signs were bright and the traffic was loud and the people on the street had a look of hunger about them, as though they had come there to be fed.

•

When he got home, he opened the door and fell against the wall, moving with the sensation of having been thrown. It had been so long since he drank seriously, he had the feeling of slipping. His thoughts skidded towards blackness. In the lounge room, he lunged for his phone and dialled Dom's number. He couldn't get a hold of his thoughts; they plunged forward, falling as though tossed from a cliff.

When Dom answered the phone, he could hear soft, lulling music in the background. A trumpet. Jazz.

'Dom, it's Andrew,' he said. His head spun and he sat down and held his head between his knees.

'Oh, hi,' she said, her voice quiet, lowered so it would not be heard by others.

'Where are you?'

'At home,' she said. The music softened into the background and he heard a door close. She was moving through the apartment they shared together and he didn't know who else was there.

'Do you have people over?' His voice sounded shallow.

'Yes,' she said. He heard a sudden ripple of laughter across the line, a chorus of it. Were they laughing at him? Had he become the joke in Dom's life? Maybe that was what he had made himself into.

'I found out more about Kirsten. I saw one of her drawings this afternoon. I just—I don't know what happened to her. No-one does really,' he said, aware that his thoughts were leaping from place to place. He stood up, but felt he was standing on sloping ground.

'Are you drunk?' she said. 'You hardly ever drink. What's happening to you?'

He didn't answer her. He couldn't really explain it. He wished he'd never come back to Sydney. He'd made a mistake in leaving Berlin and he wondered now if he'd spend the rest of his life regretting it.

'You know you've been away for a month?'

'A month?' He hadn't been counting and time had passed so easily. He had left with the intention of returning straight away yet somehow, now that he was here, he couldn't bring himself to leave.

'Sorry, I didn't intend for it to take this long. I went to the coronial inquiry into Kirsten's death here, remember I was telling you I needed to stay for it? It finished early. Not even her mother really knows what happened to her.'

'I've been back in Berlin for almost two weeks now,' she said, and there was a flatness to her words.

'She was just such a talented artist,' he heard himself saying. 'She was much better than me, you know.' Even as he spoke, he knew this, all of it, wasn't only about Kirsten, that somehow it was to do with him. 'She could draw. Just with her hands.' He said this as though the ink she had used had bled from her fingers. He felt tears on his skin, hot tears that dripped all the way down his cheeks and from his chin.

Something changed then in Dom's voice. All the patience was expelled from it and it became thin and hard like steel. 'What's happened to you? Have you fallen in love with a dead woman?' He heard a clink, the sound of her putting down her glass of wine. It was a definite sound, a certain one—inside her, something had come to an end.

'No, that's not it.'

'Andrew, I'm thirty-nine and I love you and you are a difficult man to love.'

He didn't know how to answer her. Of course he loved her, but there were things he also had to know about himself. He'd become so used to keeping quiet in his life that it was difficult for him to speak openly and find a way to explain himself to her.

22

Andrew went to his mother's house to borrow her library card. There was a cool breeze blowing over Sydney from the ocean and a salt tang in the air. She kept the library card under the small bowl on the kitchen bench and he went into her house while she wasn't there and took it without asking. He went to the library at Leichhardt, knowing it was where Pippa worked, hoping to see her there.

The photographs of Phoebe were still on a USB stick sitting on a bench in his apartment. He hadn't sent them off to London yet. When he woke up each morning and thought of them, a tangle of nerves awoke in him as he wondered what he should do with them. He hoped that seeing Pippa now might help him make up his mind.

He also wanted to borrow a book on Diane Arbus. He remembered having bought a catalogue from a Diane Arbus exhibition the first time he'd seen her work exhibited at the Museum of Modern Art in New York, when he was still a young man, but he hadn't found it in any of his boxes in storage. He must have taken it with him to Berlin.

There was something about her photographs, about the way Diane Arbus saw people, that he wanted to revisit. His need was specific and immediate. Sometimes he thought every photograph he had ever produced was in homage to her work: the strange people, the freaks, the oddness in the ordinary. The first time he'd seen one of her photographs it had reached in and stroked his bones. Seeing her pictures, he'd realised that everybody felt this way, this dislocation, though some people were better at pretending they didn't.

He crossed Norton Street and walked through the arcade to the Italian forum, through the walls and floors of terracotta, descending the stairs to the library.

The glass doors parted with a sudden jerk and he was hit by the quietness inside; the absence of sound had a pull to it, a seduction. It drew him into it. He moved towards the closest shelf, but it was full of children's picture books. Some of the names he recognised from his childhood: *The Very Hungry Caterpillar*, *Where the Wild Things Are* and *Possum Magic*. He would lose himself in the pictures and forget about the words.

The library smelt of ageing paper. The ceilings were low and the light was fluorescent and sharp. As he walked deeper into the room it felt like a bunker, a place protected from the outside world. He had forgotten this about libraries—that, like galleries, they were places in which quietness is encouraged.

He found the non-fiction shelves and stood in front of the books. It had been such a long time since he'd had to sort through books, to check a catalogue and to sift through information. When he couldn't find a shelf of photography or art books, he walked to the counter. Pippa was standing right there with her head down and her brown hair falling across one shoulder. She looked up.

He smiled at her, wondering if she would remember him.

'Hi Andrew,' she said, her voice throaty and warm.

'Hi,' he replied. Above him a fluorescent light stuttered. 'How are you?'

'I'm well. I thought you'd have left Sydney by now?'

'Yes, I was supposed to, but something came up.'

'You certainly made a big impression on my daughter. She has it in her head now that she wants to be a photographer.'

'Really?' he said, feeling giddy as his thoughts struck Phoebe again. Soon he would be leaving for London, where the photographs he'd taken of Phoebe would be hung on crisp, white walls and people would stand and frown at them and appraise her image. The more he thought about it, he couldn't see how the photos could be shown without causing some damage to her.

'Actually, her birthday's coming up. She'll be twelve next week. She asked me for a camera.' She held her mouth in a strange shape after she spoke, as though attempting to anticipate his reaction to what she'd said. 'But I'm just not sure which one to get for her.' She shook her head, remembering where she was and moved closer to the computer. 'Are you looking for something?'

'I'm after a book about the photographer Diane Arbus.'

Pippa typed something into the keyboard. 'It looks like we have a biography and a book of her photographs. They should both be on the shelf.' She moved out from behind the counter and he noticed again how short she was. He stood over her, feeling too tall in her presence and stooping slightly, like a giant, as they stood beside the shelf together. She deposited two books in his hands.

'I'll leave you to decide,' she said and padded back towards the front counter.

'Thanks,' he called after her.

He flicked through *Diane Arbus: Revelations* and as he looked at the photographs, the rest of the world became a soundless, watery pool. There was something about looking at a photograph that made him hold his breath, drawn suddenly into the moment of the image. He flicked through the book and stopped at *The Backwards Man*. The photograph was of a man standing fully dressed in a bedroom. He looked perfectly ordinary until you saw his feet were facing in the opposite direction to his body. At first it appeared to be a sleight of hand, a photographer's trick, but the longer he spent looking at the photo the more the man appeared normal. A photograph could do this: it could make strangeness seem normal and transform it into a thing of beauty. He had been thinking more and more that maybe this was what a photograph was for.

When he walked back to the counter to borrow the book, Pippa was serving another customer. Above him, the air conditioning hissed as he waited.

'Find what you were after?' Pippa asked when it was his turn.

He nodded. 'Yes, I did. Thank you.' He took his mother's library card from his wallet and slid it, together with the book, across the counter.

She picked up the card and looked at it for a moment, hesitating.

'It's my mother's card,' he said. He thought she was probably the type of person who struggled with breaking rules.

'Oh, okay,' she said and smiled tightly. There was a beep as she scanned the card's barcode. She held on to it for another moment, weighing it in her hand.

'I don't suppose you'd be able to help me decide what sort of camera to buy for Phoebe? I find the technical details in the catalogue confusing and I want to make sure I get one she can use.' She didn't quite meet his gaze as she said this.

'Sure,' he said, surprised by her question, that she would trust him with this. She struck him as a person for whom it was difficult to ask for help. She pushed the Diane Arbus book back across the counter to him.

'I have a catalogue in my bag,' she said, nodding over her shoulder towards the mirrored glass behind her, where he saw a dark shape moving. 'I finish work in about fifteen minutes.' She sounded hopeful.

'Well,' he said, looking at his watch, 'I could get a coffee and wait for you?'

'There's a café just up the stairs.'

•

It was a Tuesday afternoon and the café was empty, apart from two old men in the corner speaking Italian loudly. The walls and furniture were an off-white, discolouring unevenly like old teeth. He sat in the café that smelt of garlic and red wine and realised how hungry he was. Lately, there was a space in the pit of his belly.

Pippa walked past the front window with a library bag over her shoulder weighed down with books. She wore a scarf tied loosely around her neck. On her way in, she gave the door a heave, but it offered very little resistance and swung inwards quickly. Her movements were flinty and determined. There was a seriousness about her; she was ready to attend to business, not wanting to waste any time. She dragged a chair from the next table to his and already had the catalogue out of her bag when she took a seat opposite him.

'Would you like a coffee?' he asked. He'd already started sipping at his, a warm, syrupy liquid.

'Oh yes,' she said. She pushed the catalogue across the table towards him then went to order a coffee for herself. He flicked through the glossy brochure, but found the number of cameras inside overwhelming. It had been a long time since he'd had to make a decision about a new camera. He'd used the same Hassleblad for over ten years and only bought a new, updated model a few years ago, with an influx of money from a successful exhibition. He liked this certainty, that it was settled and he no longer had to make a decision about this important aspect of his work.

Pippa walked back to the table, watching her cup as she walked. He had the brochure closed when she sat down.

'Where's Phoebe today?' he asked.

Pippa lifted her head, but didn't quite meet his gaze. 'She's staying with her father tonight.' He saw that the mention of Phoebe's father caused her some discomfort. She took a sip of her coffee. The lines around her eyes were set like scores in pastry.

'You must have been young when you had her?'

She looked up at him quickly. 'I fell pregnant when I was twenty-two. Her father and I separated before she was born.' She smiled with the self-consciousness of a person unused to talking about herself. He made the calculation. She was younger than he was by about two years yet he had assumed she was the older. She sat on the edge of her chair, looking at the wall behind him more than she was looking at him. He could see from the way she sat that she was someone who didn't allow other people into her life very easily and he was threatening to open a door that was more comfortably left closed.

'It hasn't been easy for Phoebe. Sometimes I think it's hard for children of single parents.' She stole a quick glance at him and looked to be worried that she'd given too much of herself away.

'But you two have a great relationship,' he said.

'Sometimes I think we're too close. I guess I was really too young to know how to bring up a child alone,' she said. Her sudden honesty made him look away. They didn't speak for a minute or two; the intensity of her words required a period of silence to pass between them.

He was the first to speak. 'While I was looking through the catalogue, I remembered that I actually have an old camera I could give to Phoebe. It's a very good camera, just an old model. She's welcome to it, though it's probably more sophisticated than what she needs.'

'Oh, no,' she said, holding up her hand. Like him, she had made a point of doing things on her own, and he wondered why they were both people who found it difficult to rely on others.

'No, really, it's fine. It's just sitting at my mother's house. I haven't used it in years.' Where had this sudden generosity come from? He wasn't usually a person who gave away his things. The few possessions he had acquired and accumulated, he normally kept for himself, even if he never used them.

'Well, I can pay you for it. Just let me know how much.'

A man and a boy in school uniform walked in and stood in front of the gelato freezer. The boy was wearing brown sandals and Andrew suddenly felt for him, thinking how the boy would probably be teased about those shoes at school.

'No,' he said. 'Don't worry. Honestly, I won't use it again.'

She dipped her teaspoon into her coffee, stirred and pulled it out and tapped it twice on the rim of her cup. 'When's the exhibition?'

'The end of next week,' he said. For such a long time it felt a long way away and now it was upon him, he felt the sensation of hurtling towards a wall.

He hesitated over his next words, the question he had come here to ask, unsure if it was even worth raising with her now, given his own indecision about exhibiting the images. 'I didn't hear back from you after I sent the photographs of Phoebe. I wondered what you thought of them.'

'No, I didn't get back to you, did I? I guess I was in two minds about it and then I just acquiesced. They were very impressive, I have to say.' Pippa sighed and looked away from him. 'Phoebe liked the photographs—she was fascinated by the image of herself. She kept getting them out of the drawer to look at them. She's starting to think about her appearance. I suppose it is her age.' Pippa looked down at the table and drew her finger across it in an arch. 'And, I don't know, I couldn't bring myself to say "no". Part of me thought it could be good for her self-esteem. She never seems aware of her face, but I'm worried that as she becomes a teenager, she could become very self-conscious about it.'

It hurt him to hear this. He knew that a photograph could never really help a person with their self-esteem. Maybe this was all he needed to know. He could protect her from exposure by withholding the photograph from the exhibition.

'What do you think people will say about it, at the exhibition?' She sat forward in her chair, the position of someone who is anxious. He knew it well.

'I don't know. I can never predict what the response will be.' He didn't tell her that he might not exhibit them. He didn't want to think he might have put Pippa and Phoebe through all this for no reason.

Pippa fiddled with her silver bangle, turning and turning it around on her wrist. 'I'm glad it's happening so far away. I'm not sure how it would affect Phoebe, if she knew she was being criticised.'

'Well,' he said slowly, 'keep in mind that any criticism would be directed at me rather than at Phoebe.'

'I know. I can't protect her from everything,' she said, looking away, and he understood that she wished she could.

Maybe it was the fact that Phoebe wasn't there that gave him the courage to ask the question, finally. 'How did it happen?'

'You mean her face?' Pippa's mouth was hard.

He nodded.

'I was so young when I had Phoebe. Her father and I, we drank too much tequila one night at college and I fell pregnant. We weren't in love. Back then, I was someone who used to be able to have fun. I suppose a lot has changed about me since. I was studying law at the time, you know?' Her face was slack, as though it still caused her some pain to speak of this. 'I wanted to work for the DPP after I graduated. I dropped out of law when I found out I was pregnant. I only managed to finish my arts degree. I guess I always thought I'd go back one day, but now that seems unlikely.'

'It's never too late.' He hoped his words didn't sound feeble.

'No,' Pippa said vaguely. 'Well, her father—I don't know how to put this any other way: he wasn't the man I would have chosen to start a family with. It was one night and I got pregnant and I decided to keep the baby, even though we were both young. I told him he didn't need to be involved.

'Afterwards, when Phoebe was a baby, I didn't want

her to see her father. But I knew that when she grew older and started school, she'd begin to wonder about him. I knew that I couldn't keep him from her, that it wouldn't be fair.' The way she said the last word, the way her other words seemed to halt around it, made him aware that fairness was something that was important to her.

'He was just irresponsible, but he did try. He really did try to be a good father to her. And it didn't go as badly as I thought it might, so I let Phoebe start staying with him overnight. Then over weekends.' It struck him that what she was saying was something she hadn't told anyone else, but had thought about over many years. Her words had an evenness, a pacing, that suggested she had already put them in order in her own mind.

'I'll never forget that day. It changed everything, even more than having Phoebe. That day set the course for the rest of my life. A friend and I drank a bottle of wine together in the sun on Bronte beach. It was the first warm day of the year. It had been so long since I'd been able to do anything like that and I felt, I don't know, reckless. The way I used to feel before I had Phoebe, when I only had myself to worry about. Him taking Phoebe, it was the first time since having her that I had more time to myself.'

'That sounds natural to me,' he said.

'When I walked in the front door that afternoon, the phone was ringing,' she said. 'And I knew. It was the doctor from the hospital. I was her legal guardian and they needed my permission to operate.'

'What happened?' he asked. He felt he was tilting in a direction he hadn't expected to go.

'He had let her ride in the back of a ute on his parents' farm. She fell out when he was driving in a paddock and hit her head on a rock. She was knocked unconscious. A nerve in her face was damaged and they tried to repair it, but they couldn't.' Pippa looked at him with a resolute face, as if expecting to be blamed.

'Oh, that's awful,' he said. 'But it wasn't your fault.' He said this firmly, as though his words were capable of changing something as large and painful as what she had told him. Even as he spoke he knew that what had happened was something that could only ever be mended inside her, and it was something that might not ever mend at all.

'I don't know. People do things. Things they don't intend. It can cause just as much damage to a person. Maybe in some ways the things people do unintentionally are more difficult to understand,' she said and her words resonated long after she'd spoken them, like the striking of a bell.

23

That afternoon at home, as he flicked through the pages of the Diane Arbus book, his telephone rang on the table beside him.

'Hi, Andrew. It's Renee Rothwell speaking.'

'Oh, hi,' he said. He felt himself clench. He hadn't expected to hear from Kirsten's mother again. When he had left her house that day, he had the impression that he'd been filed away in her life, like an unpleasant task she had completed once and would never have to repeat.

'How are you?' she asked, but her words sounded perfunctory, a necessary segue to something else.

'I'm fine, thanks.'

'I wasn't sure if you'd still be here. I thought you said you were heading back to Europe,' she said, pausing.

He wasn't about to explain to her the problems he was having with Dom or his exhibition. 'You see, they just called me. From the coroner's court. I thought you might like to know. The coroner handed down her findings. You can read them on the website.'

'Thanks for letting me know,' he said.

She didn't respond, but he could hear her breathing. She was lingering, as though there was something else she wanted to discuss.

'I haven't read them myself yet,' she said and gave a small, nervous laugh, a girl's laugh.

'Well, I'll get online straight away,' he said, anxious to hang up the phone and read the findings for himself.

'Yes, okay,' she said, hesitating. 'Goodbye.'

He ended the call and turned on his laptop. He went to the coroner's website and found the decision straight away. What he wanted were definite answers. He wanted a fixed point that he could look at and distance himself from. What he wanted most of all was to be told that what had happened was somehow inevitable, that Kirsten had always been this way and he couldn't have done anything, all those years before, to have prevented it. But the word that was used was *inconclusive*, an uncertain word that hovered between two places.

The coroner said that Kirsten had most likely died by asphyxiation caused by drowning, although her body was never found. She appeared to have taken an indeterminate amount of Xanax, which may have contributed to her death. The coroner couldn't rule out *misadventure*. *Misadventure*—it sounded like an ordinary and harmless word.

Andrew scanned the document again. What he read was expressed in words that were conditional, they brushed across the surface of what had happened that day at Lake George and closed over no holes. The coroner didn't delve into why a person might have died so silently; that question was left for the people who knew her and remained.

He moved to his window and below him the street looked closer than he expected it to, a small leap to the ground. There was one thing left he could do now to find out about Kirsten. He could drive to Canberra and speak to Kirsten's sister. Kirsten had driven up and down her sister's street in Ainslie that day, pacing like a person trying to gather the right words to say.

He would visit Kirsten's sister. There was more to what had happened than was contained in the coroner's report and, since her mother had said so little, maybe her sister could tell him what he needed to know. He hired a car that day.

•

Andrew had forgotten that drive out of Sydney, how the suburbs continued on and became at first older and then newer and finally more spread out the further he drove from the centre of Sydney. The houses might have been spun in a centrifuge and dispersed that way. When he was cruising out along the highway, he remembered why he liked driving, aware of the movement, of seeing the world slide silently by, the feeling of being sealed off from it and all that mattered was his destination.

The further south he drove, the land seemed to change from green into a paler colour, the landscape yellow and parched. Closer to Canberra, in a creek that ran beside the highway, willow trees grew from the water, deposited there by banks that had collapsed under their own weight. In the water their leaves billowed out around them.

He started to see on the sides of the road dead creatures bundled up like sacks. At first he didn't understand what they were until he saw a creature that must have died that day, the long pink smear of it along the surface of the road. He swerved to avoid it and the car beside him honked loudly. There seemed to be too many of them, little brown bundles on the shoulder of the road where the bitumen was soft.

•

When he reached Canberra, he had an immediate sense of the city's spaciousness. The streets were long and wide, with gentle curves, as though to accommodate a procession. There was nobody out on the streets, though, and it felt like a town that had been built but abandoned. Everything that happened in Canberra seemed to take place behind closed doors, in meeting rooms or malls. It was a city in which the streets had been planned before the buildings and houses, a giant thoroughfare designed for ease of movement from one place to the next. A place in which nobody actually stopped.

On his way to Ainslie, he stopped beside Lake Burley Griffin. The water was as dull and unmoving as a flat piece of rusted tin. It had been such a long time since he had been there and he wanted to get a sense of the city, this small, quiet place from which his country was governed; a place he had seen most often as a thin and static background on the news. He parked beside a tree with leaves that were red. In the lake, the water was a milky-brown colour, thick and silty like the water in a dam. A fountain dispersed a stream of water that was pushed sideways in the wind.

Across the lake stood Parliament House, its windows darkly tinted like those of a limousine. The Australian flag snapped on its mast in the wind. His gaze moved to the National Gallery, where Kirsten had told her mother she was going on the day she came to Canberra, and he understood why she might have decided not to go inside after all. He had felt the suffocating effect of looking at art when he was producing none of his own.

•

He drove to Ainslie along a straight road that led to the War Memorial, a monolithic arch of concrete built to honour the dead. He turned left towards Mount Ainslie, where the houses seemed to press up against the hill making the suburb feel enclosed.

When he reached Campbell Street, the street that Kirsten had driven up and down that day, a sudden shiver moved through his body. He was driving the same route she had, following the path of a woman who was now dead, the trail left behind by a ghost. It seemed to him that what she had been doing that day, driving around Canberra, was looking for a reason to live—and she hadn't found it there. She hadn't found it anywhere.

He braked and the car behind him, large in the rear-view mirror, sounded its horn. The sudden noise unsettled him. On the letterbox beside the car, he saw the number he had parked beside was forty-eight; the house he was looking for was number fifty-two. The handbrake was stiff, resisting as he pulled it into place and he waited in the car, knowing that as soon as he stepped outside, he would have to make an investment in what he had come to do. He extracted the keys from the ignition, stepped out of the car and breathed in air that was cool. Gum trees lined both sides of the street and they had outgrown it, set to a different scale than the houses in the suburb.

Number fifty-two was a single-storey, cream-brick home, as neat and compact as a model. There was a clean, white car parked outside the double garage. It was the sort of house that gave away nothing about the people who lived inside it and offered him no sense of what to expect.

As he crossed the lawn, dried gum leaves crunched under his shoes like snail shells. He rang the doorbell, and waited, but couldn't hear any movement from inside the house. He had a sudden need to leave. What could this woman really tell him about Kirsten that he didn't already know? But before he could leave, the door opened.

The woman standing before him wore a white shirt, the top button undone to reveal a silver pendant. She had her mother's awkwardness and her lips were pursed, as though in response to an insult delivered many years before. Her arms were lean and toned—she was someone who worked to look thin. She frowned at his appearance at her door.

'Yes?'

'Hello, my name is Andrew Spruce. Are you Lydia Thomas?'

The woman folded her arms, nodded, and scepticism moved across her face, a quiver of movement like someone suddenly aware of the cold. He wondered if she thought he was there to sell her something. And perhaps in a way he was seeking something from her, some reassurance that he was not to blame for her sister's death. That what had happened to Kirsten was not in any way attributable to him. He wanted someone who knew Kirsten better than he had to touch him on the arm and tell him that he was not responsible. He thought of Kirsten's death and the first feeling to surface in him was guilt.

'I know this might sound strange to you, but I met your mother last week,' he said, thinking the woman would soften at the mention of Renee. But instead he saw something else—a stung look; the look of someone unexpectedly hit with bad news. But she recovered herself quickly and he had the impression that she had grown used to controlling her own emotions.

'Did my mother tell you to come here?' she asked, and he had another glimpse of Renee in her daughter, the way her face was so carefully held. It looked as though she had tried but never quite succeeded in leaving her mother behind. Every day she would see Renee staring out from her own reflection.

'No,' he said. 'Nothing like that. I just wanted to talk to you about your sister.'

She didn't respond immediately, but finally she said, 'Kirsten.'

'Yes,' he said and worried for a moment that she might be about to shut the door on him, to turn him away. 'I used to know her. I was Kirsten's boyfriend. We lived together when we were at university.' He felt he was pushing his words up a very steep hill.

Lydia looked to her left, aware of someone else in the house, although it seemed silent to him, clean and undisturbed.

'You had better come in,' she said. The under-standing of who he was and how he was connected to Kirsten seemed to tug at her. Her shoulders slumped; a sudden new awareness of gravity seemed to weigh her down. She stepped back and let him in. He followed her into the lounge room and sat on a sofa of soft, beige leather that gave way underneath him too easily. He fell backwards into it.

Lydia disappeared into the other room and he heard the murmur of voices. A few moments later, a man walked down the hall and out the front door. He heard a car start and drive away. Lydia returned and sat on the chair opposite him. 'My husband,' she said and waved her hand in the direction of the door.

'I don't think I saw you at the coronial inquiry,' he said.

'No, I didn't go to Sydney for it,' she said. She held her hands out on either side of her body, touching the lounge with the tips of her fingers, as though to assist her with balance.

'Your mother didn't mention me to you? I went over to her house.'

'My mother and I don't talk regularly anymore,' she said, and there was a directness to her words, a finality, that made it clear the subject was closed. He wondered what it would be like, to shut a parent out of your life. He imagined that it was a door that wouldn't close easily.

'Did you have much contact with Kirsten?' he asked.

'Off and on. She lived with us for six months last year. She was looking for work down here. After she—when she stopped working for the barrister.' *The barrister.* There

223

was something about the way Lydia said those words, holding them up between them like soiled clothes.

She looked at him, regarding his clothes and shoes, appraising him. 'But we hadn't spoken in months.' Her eyes were sharp and her mouth was narrow, giving him the impression that it was taking a great deal of effort to keep her feelings at bay.

'Well, I can't imagine what it must have been like. I don't have any siblings myself.' His words made him sound like the coward he was. He looked down after he spoke and the carpet under him was the colour of crushed eggshells. 'Well,' he said, 'I know we never met, but Kirsten often spoke about you. I know you were important to her.' His skin went tight and he realised how cold it was inside the house. It must have been the air conditioning. It was colder indoors than it had been outside. 'We fell out of touch in the last few years,' he said, when she didn't respond. He worried that his words sounded too thin and superficial, that they had been said too often before by other people. It was hard for him to swallow, his throat felt dry.

'Yes, well, it's nice to know that Kirsten still had—' she hesitated, as if not quite sure how to describe him '—people who cared about her.'

He felt a tear in his eye, large and hot and threatening to fall. Emotions were welling in his chest and expanding as though inflated with warm air. He didn't dare to move or speak, for fear his feelings might engulf him.

'Could you tell me about what she was like in the last few years?' he managed to ask, barely recognising his own voice. It quavered and leapt between words.

Her sigh before she spoke was long and draughty. 'When she was well, she was fun to be with. Maybe I remember that most because I knew how dramatically things could change. You can give so much of yourself to another person; I didn't know that.' She looked up at the ceiling as she spoke and he had the impression she'd forgotten he was there when she continued. 'Sometimes, especially in those months she was living with us, I started to worry that if I kept giving she would take everything I had. To be honest, the day I came home from work and found she was gone, I actually felt relieved. Having her here almost destroyed my marriage.' As she sat opposite him, she looked guarded and composed and not very much like a generous person.

'Do you know if she was getting treatment?'

Lydia shook her head sadly. 'It never really helped. For as long as I can remember, Kirsten had problems with anxiety. This was before the term was as popular as it is now. Even as a teenager, she just used to worry unnecessarily. Most of the time she was fine, but when it came it was debilitating.' She touched her fingers to her lips. 'It never did become manageable for her.'

He wondered how it was possible for him to have lived with Kirsten and not to have known that she suffered from this condition. Maybe he'd been too preoccupied with understanding himself to have ever really known anyone else. Maybe it had taken him this long in his life to begin to look outwards, to begin to understand others.

'And it was something she was very good at hiding. Mum always used to tell her she didn't have a problem, that everyone felt the way she did sometimes.'

'Did you know Kirsten came here?' Andrew asked. 'That on the day it happened, she drove past your house several times?'

She stiffened. 'My mother told me. Kirsten was always welcome here.' She looked past him. There was a pause and the house was so quiet, it might have been located amid empty fields.

'Do you know what it was like in the end?' The way she held her mouth, the flatness with which she spoke her words, made him think she was saying something she'd been waiting a long time to say.

'Talking to her, talking to Kirsten, was like waiting for glass to break. You know that moment when you drop something and you wait to see whether or not it shatters?' She looked at him, to see if he'd understood what she had said. 'That's what it was like with Kirsten. You never knew if she would be upset by even the smallest thing. It was the same way with Mum, too, when we were growing up. We were always walking around the house on tenterhooks.' There were tears in the corners of her eyes, tears of anger more than of sadness. 'For a long time, I used to forgive Kirsten for being that way because I thought she didn't know the effect she had on other people.' She stood up and moved to the window. It was overcast outside.

On the coffee table was a *Vogue Good Living* and the house on the cover was open and airy; through the window the sky and the sea were the same effortless blue.

'I'm sorry,' he said. 'To have upset you.' He felt he had come here into her house only to reopen old wounds, injuries she thought had healed.

She smiled at him, a smile that looked sore. She unfolded her arms. 'No, *I'm* sorry . . . I wish I only had nice things to tell you about her.'

He rose to leave. When he was on the other side of the flyscreen door, she said, 'She had a difficult relationship, you know.' She cleared her throat. 'With our stepfather.'

He looked at her through the gauze of the flyscreen, wanting to know more, but she bore the expression of someone who knows something but doesn't know what to do with that information.

He walked back across the freshly mowed lawn to the hire car. The interior smelt of new plastic. He fitted the key into the ignition, but found himself unable to start the car. He wondered why Kirsten had come here that day but not gone in. He wondered whether there was something in Kirsten's life that she had come down here to share, but couldn't bring herself to speak of and so instead remained silent in her car.

He drove back to the city centre with a hard feeling in his chest, a knot of emotion that sat under his sternum. Was it possible for anyone to live without letting this hardness into their heart? Or was it something that set in with age, inevitable somehow? The streets, wide and gentle, ushering him through the city and out the other side, heading back towards Sydney.

•

Half an hour out of Canberra, past flat, open paddocks where bales of hay were rolled into balls like oversized skeins of wool, he stopped at Lake George. The water had receded, exposing the dry grass, a dirty yellow that had formed the bottom of the lake when it was full. In the distance, the brackish silver water seemed still, a body of water that did not lap at its shores.

The water in the air sharpened the definition of the hills and the trees in the distance, but left a haze over the land. Behind the lake, wind turbines twirled in large, slow circles. The movement was mesmerising, the blades swishing through the air like pinwheels under a constant breath. The air glistened with water, evaporating and condensing, forming clouds, biding its time and waiting to rain.

Beneath the lake was a reservoir of water that the lake drained into, water settled onto the grass and eventually vanished below. He thought of it under the landscape, surging, moving through channels of old rock, a dark underground sea roaring away beneath him.

'It's a bit eerie, isn't it?' A voice behind him spoke and he turned, startled. A man sat with the door open, leaning from his car, eating an orange. He hadn't noticed him there. The man had a white head of hair and a beard that covered only his chin.

'God, you gave me a fright,' Andrew said. 'It's been a while since I last came here. I don't think I've been here since I was a kid.'

'You should have seen it a year ago. Completely empty, it was just a field. There was cattle grazing out where the water is now.' The man nodded towards the lake then bit into the orange, dripping juice onto the gravel at his feet.

Andrew moved closer to a wooden post to which flowers had been taped. The petals had hardened and turned brittle and brown, like flowers used to make potpourri. The curled red ribbon that held the bouquet in place was the only colour that remained.

The man in the car closed the door. Andrew turned and watched as he reversed the car then drove away. It would have been a day like this when Kirsten had been there; a day when there were very few other people around. How long had she sat in her car? What had she thought about but been unable to say?

He looked out into the haze of refracted water. What sort of numbness would it have taken to have walked out there? There was a silence about this lake, as though the water had blunted every sound.

He stayed there for a long time, until the moon rose up over the hill on the other side of the lake. It was an early moon that was almost full and, as it climbed, the lake amplified the moon's light like an upturned spoon. This was a place in which there could be no certainty, the evaporating stretch of water, the lake that was always changing its shape.

24

On the way back through Sydney he noticed banners along William Street catching the breeze and collapsing. They were advertising the Museum of Contemporary Art's *Photography Now!* exhibition and he remembered that two of his own photographs would be exhibited there. He thought about Phoebe; maybe he should take her to see the exhibition? If she was interested in photographs, it would help her understand his profession.

There was something about Phoebe that made him curious. Her face fascinated him; he wondered how she would understand this part of herself as she grew older, what she would make of the way the world saw her and what type of person she would become because of it.

He called Pippa when he got home, and he was surprised when she agreed without hesitation to let him take Phoebe to the exhibition. On Friday afternoon, when Phoebe finished school early, he went to their house to give her his old camera and show her how to use it. When he arrived she showed him her bedroom. Her room was painted green, the colour of an apple, and the light fittings were shaped like ladies' hats. Her bed was under a window, small and narrow, and the bedspread was covered in flowers. It still looked like the room of a young girl, though Phoebe would soon be a young woman and all this would come to embarrass her.

On her desk was a photograph of her with a man he presumed was her father. They were on a farm, the field behind them a parched and distant green. They were both wearing large smiles, the smiles that come at the end of a laugh, and her father was crouched on one knee with an arm draped over his daughter's shoulder. There was something about the way her father held her there. It was an affectionate gesture, but one of ownership, as though with this photograph he was telling the world, *This child belongs to me.*

Outside in their backyard, the magnolia tree had bloomed, but it was late in the season and the flowers were loose, the petals losing their grip on the stem. The tree was large, its branches sprawling out over the fence and into the neighbour's yard, unwilling to observe the boundaries intended to contain it.

He tried to tell Phoebe what he knew about taking photographs. If he could take everything he knew and give it to her, that's what he would do. She might be the only person he had to tell about this. She might be the only opportunity he had to share what he had learnt. He thought of the similar lesson he'd been given by his father in his own backyard when he was ten. He wondered whether people were doomed to repeat these things that had happened to them earlier in their lives, to replay the things that had formed them again and again, to turn them over like stones.

A magpie landed on a branch and stared at him with its head cocked, as though doubtful of his motives. Phoebe looked up at him with an open face, concentrating on what he was saying.

'To take a good photograph,' he began, 'there are three main things you need to keep in mind. Composition—what is inside and outside of the frame. Focus, which determines where the viewer focuses their eyes. And, most important, you have to pay attention to where the light falls.'

It was hard for him to explain to Phoebe that usually he thought about his photographs for so long that by the time it came to actually taking the picture, the act of opening and closing the shutter seemed almost incidental. How could he tell her why he loved taking photographs so much? For him it was so intimately connected with loss. He told her instead about the beauty of capturing something that would never happen again.

·

Afterwards, he drove into the city in his mother's car and parked under the Opera House, spiralling down the ramp until he found a vacant space. It was the first time he had been in a public place with Phoebe and he noticed, as they walked around Circular Quay towards the museum, that people stared at her, but usually only until they noticed something wasn't right with her face and then they looked away again. Phoebe seemed either not to notice, or to be used to it.

She didn't seem to feel compelled to be always speaking and he liked that about her. She was happy to allow quietness to pass between them. For most people, silence delivered only discomfort. He found it hard to understand the endless need those people had to fill their lives with noise.

Tourists swarmed around the quay, distracted by the view and unable to walk in straight lines, snapping with their cameras and pushing the world away. The day was cool for the time of year and the air around them smelt of salt and diesel from the ferries pulling in and out of the quay. They stood for a moment and watched a man play an instrument that looked like a concave drum but sounded like a xylophone. As they watched, Phoebe leant in towards him and he could feel her body close to his. She thought nothing of closing the space between them and he realised how he'd shut this from his life, this easy intimacy with others. It had taken a child to remind him.

Beside them, the ferries floated imprecisely towards wharves and lurched against the wooden docks. On the opposite shore, houses crept up a hill, staggered one behind the other like tiered seating. They walked towards the MCA—it had been so many years since he'd been there. He loved the building, the warm evenness of the sandstone; walking inside it always felt welcoming to him. On his first visit there, he had not been impressed by the art so much as the names beside the works. He saw the dates and places where the artists had been born and died. It was a revelation to him, that these were real people. People actually did this with their lives—they made art. It was the first time he understood that if he dared to want it, there was a life in which self-expression might be possible.

As they walked into the shadowy recesses of the building, there was a long cry of a boat from the harbour, singular in tone and sorrowful, like the call of a wounded whale. As they stood in line for their tickets, Phoebe pulled out a plastic purse and a twenty-dollar note unfurled from inside it. She held it out to him, awkward and honest and beautiful.

'No, it's okay,' he said. 'I'll get our tickets.'

'But Mum gave me the money,' she said, looking at

the note in her hand. The right side of her face made a small, slipping movement.

'Maybe you'll see something you like at the shop when we come out,' he said.

As they walked through the exhibition, he found himself checking on her now and then, making sure she was within sight, convinced that nothing bad could happen to her as long as he could lay his eyes upon her.

On the ground floor was a series of Tracey Moffatt photographs. They passed the self-portrait of her looking coyly out from the image, the saturation of red, yellow and blue and the background behind her that might have been painted. He had never felt he could work with such dramatic colours. To him, bright colours felt artificial.

On the next level were three Bill Henson photographs and he worried as they moved past them that Phoebe was too young to be looking at them, the nakedness of them and the suggestion of sex they had about them. He had a sudden urge to cover her eyes with his hands, but maybe they suggested carnality to him and to her they suggested something different.

He stood for a moment and watched the people around him. This was what he loved most about galleries, the way people slowed down in order to look at art.

In the next room, there were two photographs by Loretta Lux, dream-like pictures of children who looked like incorrectly proportioned dolls. He didn't say anything when they passed his photographs. The first was *Teething* and the next was a photo he'd taken of a woman with a cochlear implant which he'd called *Silence*. In that photo, the woman was parting her hair with her hands to show where the implant had been inserted and it looked like a computer port into her head. He had wanted somehow to capture what she experienced, the total absence of sound she lived with.

He was proud of that image, of the detail of it, but mostly he was proud of its stillness. The final photograph he had produced, somehow, didn't look like her at all. It didn't even look like anything that resembled life. Instead she looked like something carved from stone.

'That's you,' Phoebe said, pointing to his name beside the photographs. His first reaction was one he knew well, but the feeling sank quickly. He wondered if this was why he had brought Phoebe there, to prove that his photographs were not the work of an amateur. That he was a professional artist.

He looked at the little white sign beside the work. *Andrew Spruce. Born 1972, Sydney.* It always surprised him that he could be reduced to so few words and that his art said more about him than any description ever could. Alongside his photographs, these were the only facts that mattered about him.

He moved into the next room and looked at a series of Nan Goldin photographs. A couple in bed, the woman naked, facing away from the man who sat on the edge of it with his chin caught in his hand. A man submerged in a bath, his nipples a ripe purple through the water; the bruised body of a man who looked to be recovering from surgery. Images of suffering and cruelty, of what it was like to live in a world populated by people who lived separately.

When he stepped back from the photograph, his eyes swept the room. Phoebe wasn't there. His thoughts accelerated from *I lost her* towards *someone has taken her.* And then he was thinking about what he would say to Pippa when he came home without Phoebe. His mind was trained this way, at rushing towards catastrophe. For him it was the closest destination.

He moved into the next room and stopped. Someone was saying his name. *Andrew*, he heard. *Andrew, Andrew.*

For a moment, through the bodies, he thought he caught a glimpse of Kirsten standing in the corner of the room, between two white walls, her hair the blackest thing in the room. Not even looking at the art, just observing people around her with small, ungenerous eyes, looking for what might cause her harm, actively seeking it out. He stepped to the side to gain a better view of the woman, but he lost sight of her. In that moment he thought he'd seen Kirsten and the look on her face was a wounded look, her stance was crooked, her body askew. He had never found out what it was that had made her that way, how she could look at the world and all she saw were its threats.

He heard his name again and orientated himself towards the sound. Through the crowd he saw Phoebe, her little handbag over one shoulder, strapped across her body, the small pocket of plastic resting above her waist. She was smiling at him and saying his name, her voice bright, like something ripened in sunlight. She was waving him towards her. When he reached her she was pointing towards a photograph, her finger almost touching the glass. He felt himself draw breath.

'I like this one,' she said. It was a photograph of a dead bird, a native parrot on a white porcelain plate, sitting on a table next to a bowl of fruit. He smiled at her, unsure what to say, troubled that she liked something that had such a connection with death, concerned that because of his own taste in art he had encouraged this in her. He didn't want to tamper with her view of the world until all she saw was its darkness.

'How about we go and get something to eat?' He found himself rubbing her back, a warm gesture, and he wasn't sure where it had come from inside him.

Phoebe nodded.

Before they left the museum, he took a last look behind him to see if he could see someone, anyone, who he might have mistaken for Kirsten. There was a young woman with dark hair wearing a dark blue dress, but she was taller than Kirsten and he saw her only from behind before she disappeared into the next room.

They walked out of the MCA towards a French patisserie he knew a few streets away in The Rocks. Outside, the light had turned thin and silken, falling over the buildings in folds.

They sat out in the back courtyard and he brushed the scattered sugar crystals from the table with the back of his hand.

'What would you like?'

Phoebe looked at the menu. The waitress waited to take her order, poised, pen over her pad. He ordered a coffee for himself. Phoebe looked at the menu and bit the inside of her cheek, unable to make up her mind.

'I'll come back,' the waitress said, looking towards another table.

'Would you like something to eat?' he asked Phoebe, feeling impatience rise in him. He was so used to being productive, to getting things done, he had forgotten that a child's sense of time is endless. He envied her for that. He could no longer live his life without the awareness that the time he had was limited.

'How about a milkshake?' he asked.

Phoebe nodded and licked her top lip.

After he'd ordered, he noticed that the other people in the café were looking at them and he could see them wondering what the relationship between he and Phoebe was. For the first time he realised that people might assume she was his daughter. He arranged himself around that thought, knowing that he was easily old enough to fill that role. If his life had turned out differently, he might have already been responsible for another human being, but he had given himself, instead, to other things.

From above, a flower from a frangipani tree fell to their table, its white petals bruised. 'How often do you see your dad?' he asked, thinking of the photograph he'd seen of them together in her bedroom. He thought of what he had seen in that picture, the sort of possessiveness in the way her father looked at her.

'It depends. It's supposed to be every second weekend and one week in the school holidays.' She spoke these words very formally, as though reciting the orders of a court. 'But sometimes he gets busy.' She didn't sound disappointed by this. It was something she had accepted long ago.

'What does he do?'

Their drinks arrived and Phoebe started playing with her straw, stirring her milkshake as though trying to decide whether it was okay to drink.

'He's an engineer,' she said, lifting her head and fitting her mouth over the straw. 'He has a girlfriend.' There was a glint of something in her eye when she said those words, an invitation for him to agree this was a bad thing.

'Do they live together?' he asked.

Phoebe nodded. He watched her milkshake lower in the glass as she drank it.

'My dad moved into his girlfriend's apartment last year, but I don't have a bedroom there, so I sleep on a fold-out couch when I stay.' It didn't sound like this was something she resented.

'Does your mother have a boyfriend?' he said and felt himself turn red, worried she might think he had some interest in Pippa.

She shook her head resolutely, as though she thought this was the proper order of things.

'Did you enjoy the exhibition?'

'I liked it, but I still don't know what makes one photograph better than another.' Her mouth hovered over her straw as she spoke.

'That's a good question. Even I don't always know. Sometimes it's the composition, or the idea behind it. Almost always it has something to do with light.'

She lifted her straw from the glass and licked it clean.

'I want to be a photographer,' she said loudly, hopefully, and then looked back into her lap, recoiling from the strength of her own words.

'Really? You don't want to be something else? Like a doctor or a vet?' he said, hearing his voice high and jangling, jostling for a sense of control over his feelings. He wanted to take her firmly, hold both her arms and say *don't. Don't do what I did with my life. Don't make your career so bound up with who you are at the expense of everything else. Do something that matters to other people.*

'I think so,' she said less decisively, looking at him for some sort of encouragement, but he couldn't bring himself to give it, knowing what sort of a life it might mean for her.

They drove home down Parramatta Road in his mother's car and the sun was in his eyes. He folded down the sunshade, feeling exhausted. Being with Phoebe was draining. She absorbed so much of his attention, more than he was used to giving over to another person. The traffic started and stopped and he tried not to tap his fingers against the steering wheel or show his impatience to get her home.

When they finally pulled up outside her house, Pippa opened the door almost immediately, as if she had been watching for them. The way she looked at that moment reminded him of a bird, with bright, darting eyes, sitting on a nest, aware of everything, of the way in which things could go wrong, the threats to her eggs. Phoebe disappeared behind her mother and inside the house.

'How did you go?' Pippa asked and her face looked awkward, her features bunched, as though a drawstring had been tightened behind her face.

'I think she liked it,' he said.

'Thank you for doing this,' she said, her words halting, hesitating between each one. He understood, then, that she was someone who hadn't allowed herself to accept other people's kindness very often.

'Well, I was glad I could take her.' Phoebe appeared at her mother's shoulder. He could tell already that she was going to be taller than her mother when she grew up.

'Bye, Phoebe.' He waved to her and as he saw them there so close together he felt a stab of unexpected envy.

Pippa had given her life to being a mother and, in return, she had produced this shy and glorious girl. It made the thing he had done with his life, these photographs he'd taken, seem very static and small.

'Bye,' he said to Pippa, turning suddenly, feeling he was on the brink of tears.

'Thank you,' he heard from Phoebe as he walked out to the car.

As he left, he thought of Kirsten and how she had been his only real chance at a life like this, at children and a family. It was what she had wanted, to tie herself to the world through him.

In the front garden, along the fence, was a plant with light green leaves and timid yellow flowers. They were the type of flowers that closed for the night and opened for the day in order to absorb the sunshine.

25

The phone rang on his way back into the apartment. It was almost seven and he felt a tenseness move through his body like the tightening of screws. He needed a period of silence in order to process the photographs he'd seen and the time he'd spent with Phoebe. He didn't want to be distracted by speaking to another person straight away.

'Hello?' he said sharply, hoping to make it clear to the person on the other end of the phone that he had no time to talk.

'Hello. It's Renee Rothwell speaking.'

'Hi,' he said, wondering what she had to say to him now, after the coroner's findings had been handed down, when there was nothing more that could be done. He wondered if she knew that he'd seen her other daughter, if the two had discussed him since his last visit, if she was calling to ask him to explain himself. Perhaps he was walking unknowingly into some sort of bitter domestic dispute. Outside his apartment, night had fallen.

'Well, I hope I haven't disturbed you?' she said in the same breathy voice he had heard her use before. She paused. Everything about her was poised and timed for effect. She was a woman unable to live by impulse; she interacted with the world in a very calculated manner. 'I wondered if you would have time for a coffee with me?' Her voice had a haltingness to it now; she knew she was asking him for a favour. 'I could come to you. You needn't come back all the way back over here again, I mean.'

The overwhelming feeling he had was one of curiosity. What was it she thought he could offer her now?

'Sure. What about tomorrow? Bar Coluzzi at eleven?'

•

He chose Bar Coluzzi because it was central and he thought it would be easy for her to find. But seeing her there before him, squatting on the small wooden stool so close to the footpath, he regretted his choice. She looked awkward with her legs bent up. He looked down the street and wondered if he should suggest they relocate.

'Hello,' she said when she looked up and saw him standing there.

She was the sort of woman who was used to being in an environment that was familiar to her and he could tell that finding herself there in an unknown place caused her some unease. He sat opposite her. She wore pearls and pinched the strands between her fingers, pulling each one out and shaking it, as though they were making her hot. Her handbag was on the ground beside her and she wore tan stockings that seemed out of place—too demure for Darlinghurst.

'You can put that on the table if you'd like. There's plenty of room,' he said, pointing to her handbag and moving the sugar sachets to one side of the small table between them. Behind them, a small white dog was straining on its leash.

'No.' She shook her head. The skin under her eyes was dark, bluish, like the bruise left behind by a thumb. Their coffees arrived in small brown cups and she didn't speak straight away. She took small sips, holding her cup carefully, observing him over the rim.

'Did it take you long to get here?' he asked. His feeling of responsibility for bringing her there clawed at him.

'No. Not very long. I had to come into the city anyway.' Her voice sounded as though she was thinking of a faraway place. He wondered whether he should say something about the coroner's findings, if that was what she had come to discuss with him. He cleared his throat to speak.

Renee made a small movement, slipping her hand

into her handbag surreptitiously. She left her hand in her bag as she continued to speak. 'I was on our computer last week. At home. It's my husband's computer, for work, and I don't use it very often. I found some photographs.' She paused, looking up, and he had the feeling that she wanted him to anticipate what she was about to say so that there would be no need for her to say it herself. He tipped forward on his seat.

'I printed them out.' She pulled an envelope from her handbag that was large enough for building plans. She laid it on the table.

'What are they of?' he asked. Their conversation seemed to be hovering on the border of strangeness.

'Kirsten,' she said, holding her coffee over its saucer. 'They're of Kirsten.' She spoke with her face down, her voice lowered, like some kind of admission.

'Do you know who took the pictures?' He picked up his cup and sipped, but the coffee had already lost its heat.

'I think she took them herself.'

'Herself?' He still didn't understand why Renee thought he should see the photographs. It seemed there was some crucial piece of what was taking place before him that he didn't fully comprehend.

'Yes,' she said and nodded towards them. 'I made copies. They're for you.' She started sipping at her coffee more quickly. Hurrying. 'I'd like you to have them.' She patted the envelope and withdrew her hand, as though from something hot.

He wanted to rip the envelope open immediately and see what was inside, convinced those photographs were the crucial detail that had eluded him, the thing that would help him to understand why Kirsten had acted as she did that day, why her life had taken such a wrong turn and whether it had anything to do with him. But the way they were sitting there, so carefully positioned on the small table between them, made him think he did not want to look at them in front of her. They sat together on their small stools, saying nothing and sighing, like two weary travellers crouched by a fire.

The silence grew between them and he wondered whether she was there because she wanted someone to talk to. He thought of his mother in the years after his father died, when he scuttled around the house quietly as a child, not daring to cry himself for fear of upsetting her. He thought of Renee's husband and how he had not looked like a man who was prepared to discuss things that were difficult. Maybe all Renee wanted was a witness to her grief. Someone, in other words, to cry to.

Before he could speak again she stood suddenly, the movement quick and awkward. She slipped her weight forward and stood with her feet apart, splayed like a weightlifter's.

'Thank you for meeting me,' she said, looking down at him, and something about the way her voice changed made him think that she preferred this position, that she would rather he didn't look at her so directly.

'Thank you for the photos.'

She nodded and he watched her walk to the car. It was dark and new. She was a woman who would always be driving cars that were new. She had arranged her life in order to make it that way.

•

In his apartment, he opened the envelope. The photographs had been taken at close range. Some of them didn't catch all of Kirsten's face and he thought she must have used a self-timer. They had been printed on paper and the colours were too strong, cartoonish, the ink bleeding out from the edges of her face. It was difficult to look at someone who was now dead depicted in such striking tones.

He laid them out on his kitchen table, standing over them as though he was examining a contact sheet, taking in the images one at a time, attempting to understand each photograph. He forced himself to look at her eyes first and then he moved to her mouth, the way she held it, looking for the words it was holding back. The differences between the photos were so pronounced he might have been looking at photographs of different people, except there was one thing that was consistent about each of the photos: Kirsten looked at the camera as though she wanted something from it. She wanted it to find the beauty in her.

He put the photographs back in the envelope Renee had given him; he felt that in giving these to her Renee was somehow reaching out to him. He thought of the last look she gave him, over her shoulder, a lingering look, and he knew she had something else to tell him, but it was something that was not easy for her to speak about.

26

The next day he decided to call Renee, to thank her politely for the photographs and ask her whether there was something else she wanted to say. He picked up his telephone on the kitchen table and scrolled through the recent calls to find her number. But he hesitated. He wasn't sure how to ask the question; he wasn't even sure he knew the right question. He held the phone in his hand, but didn't make the call. He watched the traffic move up New South Head Road; it was Sunday again and the cars were inching their way to the coast. He knew as he watched the cars he'd stayed here too long seeking answers; maybe there were no answers. He should book his flight to London.

Since he'd been back in Sydney he'd already visited all the galleries he used to see in Darlinghurst and Surry

Hills. He'd been to the museums, but he'd found nothing he could stand in front of and lose himself inside. What he would give now to see a Rembrandt. On his last visit to the Rijksmuseum, when he'd travelled to Amsterdam from Berlin for a group show, he had finally worked out what it was he loved about Rembrandt's paintings. It was his sparing use of light. He spent hours standing in front of paintings, perfectly still, allowing them to seep inside him.

The darkness of them, the paint thick, coating the canvas like molasses, the emphasis placed on people, on their expressions, the way they looked at one another and out of the frame. The artist had used light to illuminate people's faces and offer a glimpse into their thoughts. A painter he'd met at an artist's residency had said the reason Rembrandt's paintings had that darkness to them was because he primed his canvases with black paint. He wondered sometimes what Rembrandt would have made of a camera. He had the sensibility of a photographer, the same feeling for light.

●

In the afternoon he went swimming at a pool near St Mary's Cathedral. He walked down William Street against the tide of traffic, when the city workers were still sitting behind their desks in glass towers, shuffling their papers and tapping their keyboards. He had never known that sort of life, having to be in one place each day and being accountable to others. In the way he had chosen to lead his life he was answerable only to himself.

Inside the pool complex, the air was warm and moist, touching his skin like a sultry fog. He sat on the benches and watched the swimmers slice through the water in straight lines. The lane closest to him was unoccupied and the water there was an unbroken blue. He sat there in the chlorine air, the tang in his nostrils, a sting in his eyes. Bodies lumbered up and down lanes, arms overhead; an old man with a short stroke moved like a wind-up toy.

Why were they always painted this same colour, these pools? The permanent blue of a shallow, tropical sea, the blue of holidays, of hot sand and palm trees. A blue that was not real, that spoke of a fiction, the glimpse of the cover of a travel magazine then lost in the tumble of life. He never swam in a chlorine pool without being conscious of this, the idea that stood behind it, the thing that most people had never actually seen but spent their lives wanting.

He dived into the pool, the cool water stripping his body of its warmth. Encased in water, breathing was an effort, but about ten laps in something in him changed. His movement slowed and he was more aware of each stroke as he lifted his arms over his head and silver bubbles parted around his hands, in his ears water gurgled each time he turned his head. The light through the moving water concentrated into curling strands on the blue tiles. He wanted to take those threads of light and stretch them between his fingers. The water around him felt warm and familiar, like amniotic fluid.

When he had swum thirty laps, he emerged from the pool and showered, but the smell of chlorine remained with him, soaked into his skin. He walked outside and he was aware of the chlorine haze around him, moving with him like a personal cloud.

•

Afterwards, with the water from the pool still lodged in his ear, he went to the supermarket near his apartment. He stood in front of the olives, wondering which jar to choose. Dom would know which olives to buy. She was a person who lived her life that way, someone who took the time to enjoy what was good in life, who noticed which types of olives were best for a particular dish.

She'd never quite succeeded as a professional dancer, but she excelled in knowing how to live. These were the details in his life he had skimmed over on his way from one achievement to the next. This was what he'd never allowed himself time for. She had once brought home green olives stuffed with almonds from a delicatessen in Prenzlauer Berg. They ate most of them before they'd started cooking dinner, an assault of flavour that crept across his tongue. But he couldn't see any of those types of olives at the supermarket in Kings Cross. The stuffed green olives in jars had something bright and orange inside.

His phone rang and he fumbled for it in his bag, where it was lodged beneath his swimmers and wet towel. There was a delay after he'd answered the phone.

'Hello, is this Andrew Spruce? It's Marten Smythe speaking.'

Andrew stood still. With the sound of that man's voice, he had been summoned to a place he'd been avoiding. He had avoided thinking about his exhibition in London. It was taking place at such a distance away, he'd let it shift to the periphery of his thoughts.

'Hi,' he said. 'How are you?'

'Well, everything's fine here, we're setting up for your exhibition. There's just one thing. We're still missing the high-resolution files of the girl with the face. We received one USB stick with the other images, but the images of the girl weren't on it.'

'Oh, really?' he said. 'That's funny, I thought I'd included all of them.' He wondered if his words sounded as thin and gilded to Marten as they did to him.

'No. And the thing is, we really need them soon to prepare for the exhibition.' Marten cleared his throat. 'We're hoping to print the catalogue soon and obviously we'll need to hang the work in advance of the opening. We've already put most of the images on our website.'

'Yes, I understand. Sorry, I'm not sure what happened.' He wondered if he should tell Marten now that he was having second thoughts about exhibiting Phoebe's photograph. That he would send over something else instead.

Perhaps he could find some photograph he'd taken but hadn't exhibited. He was sure he could find a substitute among the pictures he'd taken in the last few years, even if it wasn't as good.

Instead, he found himself saying, 'Yes, I'll send them over today or tomorrow.'

'Good, thanks. We don't have much time left. We've sent out the invitations too.' He paused, as if expecting Andrew to say something. When Andrew didn't respond, he continued, 'I sent out a few thumbnails of your photos last week. I hope you don't mind. I must say, the response we received back was very positive, especially to the image of the girl with the face.'

So they had already shown the photographs of Phoebe to collectors. He looked at the back of the jar of Kalamata olives he was holding; they were marinated in balsamic vinegar.

'An important collector asked to see the catalogue as soon as it is printed,' Marten said to his silence.

'Great,' he said, feeling his face burn. He looked behind him, wondering whether there was anywhere in the supermarket he could take a seat. He felt dizzy.

Why was it that he cared so much about Phoebe? He'd taken scores of other photographs of children over the years and never so much as flinched. He felt he knew Phoebe; he cared about her. Perhaps he'd allowed himself to grow too close to her, but something about her face made him want to intervene and protect her.

'So you see, we need those files as soon as possible. Given the urgency, courier would be best, I think,' Marten said.

'Oh yes. I'll take care of it,' Andrew assured him. He'd let this go too far; he could see that now. He should have told Marten of his reservations weeks ago. Maybe this would be the final and spectacular end to his career. He could annoy an important London art dealer and never exhibit his work in that market again. The thought contained an uneasy attraction.

'And I take it you'll be here? For the opening, I mean.' Marten said, uncertainly, and Andrew detected an erosion of trust between them.

'I think so,' he said. He wasn't sure he would go. What he wanted to do now was to fly straight back to Berlin. He didn't want to bother with London at all.

'What's the date today?' he asked.

'The sixth of March,' Marten said.

The exhibition was opening in less than a week.

'Oh, right. Well, I had better get organised, hadn't I?' he said. This was not like him, he thought, this indifference. The things that had once meant something to him now felt so far away he could have been waving at them from a distant shore.

'Yes, if you could come to the gallery a day or two before the opening to check the proofs that would help us a great deal,' he said.

'Yes, I can do that,' he said, but what he felt was an

urgent need to end the call and concentrate on buying olives.

'Great, we can sort out any last minute issues then,' Marten said.

He finished the call and paid for the olives. On his way out of the supermarket, he stopped in front of a poster with black-and-white photographs printed in rows. There were names underneath the photographs like Claire, Matthew and Rachel. *Missing Persons* was written along the top of the paper in large, black letters. There was something odd about these photographs of lost people and it took him a few moments to realise that the strangeness came from the fact that in those photos the lost people were smiling. It would have seemed more natural to him if they looked sad, but of course the photos were taken at a time before these people became lost.

As he walked up the escalator, he thought about how these people were missing to those who knew and loved them, but to everyone else they were no more than strangers.

•

In his apartment, he counted the days. The exhibition was opening that Thursday, which left him barely five days. Did he want to miss this chance to exhibit in London? He could call Marten Smythe back right now and call the whole thing off.

But no, that was not what he wanted. Instead, he called the airline. The first flight he could get was three days away. He booked himself onto it and another sudden urgency rose in him. He needed to find out what happened to Kirsten and he needed to do it before he left.

27

When his mother was at work that night, he borrowed her car without telling her. He found himself thinking she owed this to him. Sometimes he thought she would always owe him some debt she could never repay, because the life she had given him felt like a weight he had to carry rather than a blessing to be enjoyed.

He drove across the Harbour Bridge and up the Pacific Highway to Gordon. He hadn't given much thought to what he would do when he got there, he wasn't sure what he would say, but he felt he was driving towards a sort of clarity; that when he reached his destination he would finally understand Kirsten, what she had done, her lingering silences and what was hidden beneath them. This was what he had come back to

Sydney to learn, and he needed to find out the truth so that he could leave again.

He parked opposite the Rothwells' house. The light from inside, through the sheer curtain in the window, was a pearled light that illuminated but did not expose. He could see the two of them through the window, sitting at opposite ends of the table, like two children on the opposing sides of a seesaw. They must have been eating dinner, their bodies tipping forwards occasionally to take food to their mouths. What did they speak of over their evening meals? Something made him think it wasn't their absent daughter, that the things spoken of at their dinner table were surface details; the type of things people spoke about when their thoughts were much more difficult.

He wanted to enter that house again, to stand between walls that were a shade short of white, surrounded by photos that suggested a pleasant family life. He wanted to know what it was about those walls that made him uneasy.

He kept thinking of Kirsten, sitting in her car at Lake George that afternoon, with no-one she could talk to but having something important to say. It was hard for him to believe that a person's life could end that way and he somehow felt the answer to the question of why was held between the four walls of the house across the road from him now.

Renee's shape rose from the dining table first. Her movements were fluid, her limbs moved along lines that were as curved and smooth as a figure skater's. She disappeared from the window and reappeared near her husband, stooping to collect his plate. For the next ten minutes, Saul Rothwell sat in that room with the lights out and Andrew could see the lights from the television wending their way over the ceiling.

Andrew was sitting with his hands on the steering wheel, holding it with both hands, and there was a tightness in his body as though the car was still moving and he was bracing for an accident. He kept his eyes on the house, worried that if he looked away, he might miss something crucial, some vital clue. Everything seemed to hold some significance: the switching off of a light, the orientation of their bodies away from the windows, the front door closed and left in shadow.

When he saw a light from beneath the garage as it opened, he glanced at the clock on his dashboard. It was 8.25 pm. The door rose and the light yawned out, shining onto the street, a corridor of light. The car moved slowly, easing from the driveway and turning smoothly onto the road. It was the same car he'd seen when Renee had visited him in Darlinghurst the day before. As soon as the taillights disappeared out of the street, he unclipped his seatbelt and stepped from the car. The night was cool and still.

There was a knocker, closed and round like a fist, and he struck it twice against the door. It made a hard noise of metal against metal. There was no sound from inside the house. Perhaps they had left together in the car.

Then Kirsten's stepfather opened the door. He

readjusted his glasses on his face and peered at Andrew as if he was trying to remember his name.

'Sorry to disturb you. We met a couple of weeks ago. My name is Andrew Spruce?' he said, trying to smile and sound as though it was natural that he was there, that he ought to have been expected.

'Oh yes, I remember. You're the old boyfriend.' Saul looked relieved that the mystery of Andrew's sudden appearance had been solved. He relaxed back into himself. 'Renee's gone out for a little while. To do some grocery shopping, I think.' It seemed strange to Andrew that he might not know where his wife had gone at 8.30 on a Sunday night.

They stood staring at each other and it occurred to him that Saul wasn't used to having visitors; that he didn't realise that the appropriate way to proceed from this point was to invite Andrew inside.

'I wondered if I could ask you a few more questions about Kirsten? I'm sorry to take up more of your time.'

'Oh yes. Yes, you can ask me about Kirsten,' he said and he pushed his glasses up his nose. He stayed standing there, as though he was expecting Andrew to ask him where they both stood.

'Should I come in?' Andrew asked.

Saul took a step backwards. 'Okay,' he said. 'Though I wasn't really expecting anyone tonight. My wife's out.'

Andrew couldn't decide whether the man's confusion was real or contrived.

He followed Saul to the lounge room, noticing a patch of pink at the back of his head where his hair had thinned. They sat down on the couch. The television was turned off and he wondered what Saul had been doing since Renee had left.

'I went to see Kirsten's sister,' Andrew said.

'Lydia?'

Andrew nodded.

'Oh yes, Lydia. We don't get to see her very often. She works in Canberra, you see. She went to university at ANU. She's quite senior in the public service.'

'It sounds like Lydia and Kirsten were quite close?'

Saul nodded thoughtfully. 'Yes, they were very close.'

'Lydia mentioned that there might be some—' he stopped and looked at the bookshelf, where the spines of the books were aligned so neatly they looked never to have been read '—some differences between you and Kirsten.' He decided that the only way to speak to this man, a man who sought to hide behind confusion was directly.

'Differences?' His cheeks were sunken, nestling into the space under his cheekbones as he'd aged. 'We had . . . Kirsten was . . .'

Andrew wondered for a moment whether Kirsten's stepfather was trying to work out how much he already knew. All he could think of was the night they had all had dinner together, the way Kirsten had jumped when Saul had said her father's name, as though in response to a threat. He felt somehow that this response and her death must be connected in a way he could not see yet. Some invisible line drew them together.

Saul finally finished his sentence. 'She was seven when we married.'

'Seven?' It took him a moment to understand that he was speaking of Kirsten's age.

'Yes. She was very upset, you know. About the divorce. Her father had only been gone for a year before we met. Kirsten couldn't move on.'

Andrew thought of the words *moving on* and how they sounded more like words that would be spoken about an adult than a seven-year-old girl.

'Lydia was better; she was three when her father left and couldn't really remember him anyway.'

'Her father lived in Townsville, didn't he?'

'For a time, yes. More recently he moved to Western Australia and was working in the mines over there. But we don't hear very much from him. He couldn't make it to Kirsten's funeral service.' Saul nodded sagely. If he had any opinion about this, he didn't disclose it. He looked at Andrew as though trying to determine whether he had said enough to satisfy Andrew's curiosity.

When Andrew didn't speak, he sighed. 'She always hoped Renee and her father would get back together. Even after Renee and I married. I mean, it didn't matter how often we told her he wasn't coming back.' He sat up straighter, as though possessed of a new idea. 'Would you like to see her bedroom? Some of her things are there. She kept them there for when she stayed here.'

'Sure,' Andrew said. He felt tired. All he wanted was to have his question answered and to leave again, but this man was speaking in circles.

They walked down the hall and Andrew felt his resolve crumble. Perhaps he was seeking to discover something that could never really be understood. When he opened the door, there was nothing about the room from which he could have identified the woman he once loved. It looked like a spare room, in which a bed had been set up for visitors.

'Oh,' Saul said softly. 'I keep forgetting that Renee took Kirsten's stuff to the charity bin last week. Sometimes I sit here, on the bed.' He moved to the bed and sat down on it, slumped. It looked like a position he had often assumed.

He imagined Renee moving through the room in a fury, picking up Kirsten's belongings, tearing things from the walls, disposing of everything that had once belonged to her daughter, losing control for a moment and then regaining her composure and walking back out into the hall.

'Did something happen to Kirsten? When she was young?' he asked. It was strange hearing those words aloud. It was something he had often wondered.

The question lingered between them.

'Kirsten and I, we didn't see eye to eye. It happens, sometimes. I wasn't her father,' he said.

Looking at Saul sitting there on the bed, Andrew thought he didn't even look like a man; he looked more like a boy.

Saul shifted. Something in him was stirring. 'After Renee and I married, I told Kirsten not to talk about him anymore.' He pressed his knuckles against each other and the grooves didn't quite align. 'I thought it would be easier for her mother if Kirsten didn't speak about her father.' Those silences of Kirsten's, so long and deep she often seemed lost in them. 'Don't tell Renee, though, will you? She doesn't know about that.' He looked up fearfully, as though telling the truth might be something that brought this clean and quiet life around him to an end.

•

Andrew showed himself out. As he walked across the Rothwells' lawn, he was thinking about silence. How it made a person skirt around what they couldn't speak of like the rim of a deep pit. The way it limited a person.

He knew now that this was what he had really seen in Kirsten that day they first met: this common trait between them. That in their own ways they were both struggling against this instinct they had not to express their feelings.

He didn't notice Renee's car parked on the street as he walked past. He had taken the keys from his pocket when he heard his name called out from behind him. He spun around and his heart gave a few hard knocks. Renee was standing at the edge of a beam of streetlight like a person trying to avoid exposure.

'I saw you sitting in your car when I drove out earlier,' she said, and he wondered how long she had been sitting there, waiting for him.

'Yes,' he said, but he didn't want to lie and he didn't want to hurt her with the truth.

'Did you speak to my husband?'

Andrew nodded.

Renee folded her arms around her waist. She was standing on the high edge of the gutter and her car was between them.

'Thank you for the photos of Kirsten,' he said.

'Did you come about those?'

He shook his head. What he thought now was maybe it was easier to understand someone else's life than it was to understand your own and maybe that was why he had come all the way back to Australia. He needed to decide what sort of a person he was. Was he a good photographer but a failure as a human being? He wasn't sure it was possible to be good at both things.

He looked at Renee and wondered whether she had ever felt this, if she was someone who had ever really tried to understand herself. Or whether she was as she appeared to be: someone who lived her life skating across the surface of the world as though it were a lake of ice.

'I still can't understand it,' she said and her voice assumed a new tone, one that was natural, honest, that he hadn't heard her use before. She must not use this voice very often in the life she led here. 'I know Kirsten always had her problems, but I always thought these sorts of things didn't happen to people like us. She never wanted for anything, you know.' She gestured to the house behind her, as though the only thing a person needed in life were these physical comforts. 'Not since I remarried, at least.'

And then she did something he was not expecting. She sat down on the grass as though the weight of her words had dragged her there. He moved around her car and sat down beside her. Through his jeans, the lawn was damp and wetness seeped through to his skin. She sat with her legs stretched out in front of her, her hands behind her, her feet loose, the way a defiant teenager might sit.

'My first marriage was hard,' she said. 'I really loved Kirsten's father. I mean, Saul—' she waved her hand behind her '—it was different with Saul. Our marriage was more . . .' She paused and sighed heavily. 'I made a good marriage.' He knew what she meant. She meant in a material rather than an emotional way. Saul had supported her, and was she wrong to have wanted that?

They were silent for a moment and he knew the less he said the better, that the natural inclination of most people was to try to explain themselves.

'The separation from my first husband affected me as much as it affected Kirsten. I was devastated by it, actually. I had to completely cut off contact with him in order to recover from it. Kirsten suffered from that, and I found I was better than Kirsten was at living behind a veneer.'

A car drove past slowly and its headlights came on.

'Do you have another girlfriend now?' she asked, looking at him.

He was surprised to hear her ask. In their previous conversations, she had shown no curiosity about his life. He looked at her, but couldn't see her face—the streetlight was too far away from them—and he almost preferred it that way, the two of them sitting there, unable to look upon each other, like two people sitting inside a confession booth.

'I love someone,' he said. 'But I've treated her unfairly. I don't know why I keep hurting the people I love.'

She sighed. 'Sometimes I think it's easier if you don't love the person you marry. Sometimes I think the more detached you are the better.' It was obvious that she was speaking of herself. 'The day they told me they'd called off the search for her body, I knew my life was over.' Her voice turned low and knowing. It was the voice of a person whose mind is made up and seeks no input from anyone else. 'When there's no more love in your life, it might as well be over.' She looked up. 'My other daughter and I, we don't speak very often anymore. She's much more savvy than Kirsten and better at looking after herself. She left home and never really came back. Saul might as well not speak to me. Kirsten was really all I had. She suffered a lot. In the past few years she was always angry at me and I hardly saw her in the end, but she did let me love her and that was all I could ask of her.'

He looked across at her and saw her eyes glistening like two dark pools. 'Her father drank, you know. He worried a lot. I see now that Kirsten had that same problem too. I guess I thought she had to learn to be less sensitive. And I thought I was the one who had to teach her that lesson. I was too hard on her. On both my daughters. Sometimes you don't realise what you're doing until after it's done.'

'What do you think happened to Kirsten that day?' he asked.

'I don't know. Somehow, I feel this would all be much easier to understand if they'd just recovered her body. I still wonder some days whether she'll walk back through the door.'

'Do you think it was deliberate? What she did?'

She shook her head, but not strongly enough to indicate disagreement. She exhaled a long draught of air. She said nothing and he felt the sadness of the large-limbed woman sitting beside him. To most people's sadness there is a sort of disbelief. Most people's sadness is a thing they try to fight; they think if they struggle with it enough they will eventually overcome it. But Renee's sadness was something different. It was a state that was permanent, that had set in like rot. She pressed her face into her hands. The street was quiet and all he could hear were the sounds of Renee beside him as she sucked back her tears.

'You know, I used to believe in God,' she said, looking upwards to where the moon was peeking out through a crescent gap in a sheet of deep blue. 'And in heaven and all those hopeful beliefs. But now what I think is that when I die, I would forgo a death and an afterlife if I could go back to the start of this life, armed with what I know now. I would relive it and I would execute it perfectly. I'd be aware of every second. I wouldn't need an afterlife. I think I could just about get my life right the second time around.'

When she'd finished speaking, she stood up in stages, pushing herself up from the grass with her hands. There was something desperate about the way she heaved herself from the lawn, lifting herself away from her strange, discordant and impossible words.

•

He drove back over the bridge and the harbour expanded out below him with a blackness that didn't seem to move.

He knew, now, about Kirsten. Was it his fault? It was true he had hurt her, but clearly her problems had started well before they met.

This uneasy attraction he felt towards Kirsten, the way he had been drawn to her, he understood where it came from now. He had mistaken the deep sense of empathy he felt towards her for love. As children they had both been made to keep silences and they took their silences with them as adults. The only difference between them was he had found a way to speak.

It was much more than a self-indulgence, this strange thing he'd chosen to do with his life; photography had kept him alive. His need to take photographs was an expression of his deep need to be heard.

28

The night before he left for London, he invited his mother over to his apartment. They hadn't spoken properly in the past two weeks. He wondered if he'd been too hard on her and he didn't want to leave Sydney while there was still this rift between them.

He was cooking a Spanish omelette; it was Dom's recipe. The trick to making a Spanish omelette, she had told him, was in the seasoning. He reached behind him for the salt and pepper grinders. He poured the eggs into the pan in long glistening strands.

His mother arrived in his apartment with a bottle of wine, which she offered to him as she walked in. It was a big thing for her to come to Darlinghurst, he knew, since she so rarely left the inner-west.

'Thanks for coming over, Mum,' he said, smiling and looking at the pan.

'Do you need help with anything?' his mother said, stepping towards the kitchen, a small, tentative step, as though the ground below her was fragile and might give way.

'No, you sit down,' he said, batting her away with a hand. Then, more kindly, 'I'm making a Spanish omelette, the way Dom taught me.'

'Have you spoken to her recently?'

'Yes. We've spoken,' he said. He didn't want his mother to ask him anything else. He didn't want to admit how angry Dom had been the last time they spoke and he worried what she'd say to him when he called her again, so he kept putting it off.

'We'd better eat soon,' he said. He was suddenly anxious for their dinner to start—the hurry he was in was for it to conclude. He didn't want to talk about his father with her again; he wanted simply to mend things with her so that he could fly away to London the next day.

He served up the omelette and dressed the salad, thinking to himself that it looked quite respectable, the eggs tanned the way they looked when Dom had made it herself. They started in silence, a silence that was still and gaping and one that he felt he needed to fill.

'The gallery has asked me to come to London a couple of days before the opening,' he said. He rarely spoke about this aspect of his life with his mother and she looked surprised to hear him mention it. She nodded and carefully manoeuvred a piece of lettuce on a fork into her mouth and pushed the rest inside with a finger.

His mother had only ever been to one of his exhibition openings, his first solo show in Sydney, and she had worn a black dress, stiff and crisp and bought especially for the event. She stood in the corner of the gallery, gripping the fabric with one hand and holding a glass of wine in the other. She favoured her right leg when she stood, tipping that way, uncertain about her own presence in the room. It was difficult for her, all the people and being in an environment in which she didn't know the rules.

'What time is your flight tomorrow?'

'It's around one,' he said. 'I'll go straight out to the airport after breakfast. The real estate agent has a tenant who wants to move in at the end of next week.'

'That's good to know it's been a worthwhile investment for you, hasn't it?'

'It has.'

She looked around at his apartment. 'The old place is still holding up.' She smiled gently. 'Have you ever thought about renovating it?'

He smiled awkwardly at her. 'Maybe when I get some more money.'

She was quiet, but he could tell there was something she wanted to say to him. He felt himself recoil from her; whatever it was, he didn't want to hear it. He wanted things between them to be easy again.

'I'm sorry I never told you about your father. I've been thinking about it a lot, since we had that conversation. At the time I was grieving and I didn't want to speak about it, not to anyone. I thought it would be easier if I just kept quiet and dealt with it myself. I actually thought that would make it easier for you when you were a boy.'

In doing that, she had damaged him. It was a surprise at thirty-seven to realise suddenly that his upbringing had been so flawed.

'Mum,' he said, feeling tears bank up beneath the bones in his cheeks. 'I do understand. I know it was hard for you.'

'God, Andrew, I'm so sorry. I didn't even see the effect I was having on you.' She looked away. Outside it was dark and on the road below him he could see a bright line of headlights moving up the hill from Edgecliff towards Kings Cross, like a row of nocturnal animals in the darkness, marching through the night.

He thought about Pippa and Phoebe. How Phoebe had been hurt, even though her mother thought she was doing the right thing. Phoebe would wear the damage on her face for the rest of her life. The only chance she had for surviving was to understand what had happened and to find some way to accept it. If she could do that, Phoebe would grow into a fine young woman; she might even flourish because of it.

'I found out about Kirsten, Mum. I went to see her mother yesterday, that's why I'm back here I suppose.

Somehow I can't help feeling that what happened to Kirsten must be my fault.' A sob rose in his throat, a large uncontrollable sound. All the feelings he had about Kirsten were held in his chest.

'Andrew, Kirsten was a very troubled woman.' He looked at her and wondered how his mother knew that about Kirsten.

'I know, but, Mum, you don't really know what happened between us. It went on for years. After I moved out from that apartment we shared, I couldn't live with her, but I kept seeing her. I'm not sure what was wrong with me. I'm selfish and other people end up hurt.'

'I knew that, Andrew. I knew you saw each other.'

'How? Did she tell you?'

'No. I guess because of the way you spoke about her and the way she spoke about you.' She lifted the edge of a napkin with her finger. 'But, Andrew, what Kirsten did, it wasn't your fault. You must know that. Her family—it was a very difficult situation. And she was very sensitive. That had nothing to do with you.'

'I don't understand, Mum. I cared about her. Why was it so hard for me?'

His mother took his hand.

'Do you think your dad's death might have had something to do with it? The fact that you hadn't got over it, you hadn't come to terms with it?'

'I don't know. Dad died years ago. I should have been over it by then.'

'I know, but grief takes a long time. I'm starting to think I will always be grieving, but that it just gets easier to live with.'

He found himself crying now, hot tears falling from his eyes and onto his omelette.

'I tried to encourage Kirsten to see a counsellor. Funny that it never occurred to me I should see someone myself.' His mother tore a piece of bread in her hands as she spoke.

'I left without saying anything, Mum. I didn't say goodbye. I slunk away to Berlin and never spoke to her again; I don't know what she thought. What if it was my fault, Mum? Why couldn't I have been kinder?'

'People also have a responsibility to themselves. Not everything's your fault, Andrew. Not my grief. Not Kirsten's death.' She sighed.

He looked up at her, at his mother, who'd come through a difficult thing and was suddenly wise about the world.

'You can't know why someone does something like that, Andrew. Whatever her problems were, they were bigger than you.' She paused and cut a piece from her omelette. 'Have you ever thought that maybe in those years you spent with her, you actually helped her? That maybe you helped keep her alive?'

He tilted his head back to try to stop the tears from falling. He hadn't cried like this since he was a young boy and it felt childish to lose control in this way.

His mother came over to him and they moved together to the couch. She took him in her arms. He couldn't remember ever being held so tightly by her. It took him almost half an hour to empty himself of tears and when it was over he felt calm.

Later, he showed her out and she stood in the hall for a moment, lit from above by the halogen lights, small, pursed circles. He kissed her soft cheek goodbye.

•

After his mum left, before he went to bed, he made a call to Dom.

'*Hallo?*'

'Dom, it's me,' he said.

'Hi,' she said.

'Sorry I didn't tell you sooner, but I'm flying to London tomorrow for the exhibition opening. I'll be back in Berlin a few days later.'

She sighed. 'So, now you're coming back?' Her words were short and hot, delivered like blows.

'Yes, probably on Saturday,' he said, speaking quickly, making the most of this new certainty that possessed him. 'Or, I was thinking you could come to London for the opening? We could spend a few days there. We've never been to London together, it might be fun.'

'Come to London?'

'Yes, for the opening. You usually come to my

openings with me.' It was always comforting having her there, a reminder of who he really was.

She was silent and so he continued to speak.

'I found out about Kirsten, what happened to her. And I took those photos I was telling you about, of the young girl. They'll be in this exhibition—I'm really happy with them. I think it's my best work for a long time. I'd love for you to see them.'

'I don't even know what to say. You've been away for weeks—am I supposed to ignore that? Should I pretend nothing's happened?'

'No, Dom, it's not . . . It was just . . . I'm sorry.'

'Sorry? Sorry isn't enough right now.'

'I found out about my father while I was here. How he died. It was a brain aneurysm; my mother finally told me about it. Do you know I always thought it was a heart attack?'

'Your father? How could you not know that, how your own father died? Didn't you ever ask?'

'No, Dom, I never asked my mother about it. Not until now.'

'Well, I'm glad you found out, then.' She was silent, but she didn't hang up. 'Sometimes it's very hard to know what you feel about things, Andrew. I had no idea you didn't know about your father's death.'

'No, I didn't tell you. I think I was embarrassed about not knowing.'

'Sometimes, it's like you push your feelings away.'

He paused. 'Maybe I do. But not my feelings about you.'

'No, not about me, but other things. And it affects me.'

'Don't say that. I love you. I'm coming back. I've only been gone a month—nothing's really changed, has it?'

'No, but I don't think I can do this thing where we're together, but you keep so much to yourself. If you want me to be a part of your life, you need to involve me in it. I don't want to feel like I'm living with someone who doesn't let me all the way in.'

There was a gentle click and then nothing. The silence of a dead line. Had he ruined it? He had found out about Kirsten and about his own father, but he worried that it had been at the expense of his relationship with Dom.

29

The evening of his opening in London, Andrew opened the wardrobe in his hotel room and took out his plastic suit bag. From inside, he took out his check business shirt, one of the only two formal shirts he owned and kept for occasions like this. The collar was very stiff. He unfolded the ironing board and pushed the plug of the iron into the wall socket.

He moved to the kitchenette and filled a glass of water from the bathroom tap, dipping his finger into it and sprinkling the droplets over his shirt. He pushed the warm iron across the fabric and the smell of warm cotton rose to him. There was something clean and reassuring about that smell; he smoothed out the creases of his shirt and prepared himself physically for what was to come.

He manoeuvred his arms into the sleeves, one at a time, the fabric was warm and dry and against his cool skin, it made him shiver. He moved out the door of his room and took the elevator to the lobby, where he waited for the cab. He sat on an old leather couch as firm as a muscle and watched. How much of his life had he spent this way, sitting still in order to observe other people?

In the corner of the lobby an old couple sat quietly at a table. There was a calmness around them, a stillness. Their hands were clasped on the tabletop. They didn't need to speak to each other. They were content, aware that the time they had left with each other was limited, that they had no more time to waste.

The bellboy waved to let him know the cab had arrived.

Outside the cold air grazed his lungs. He hopped in to the small black cab.

'Hoxton, please,' he said.

Was it jet lag? As they drove, everything around him looked small, the buildings and the houses like scale models of something much larger. Above him was a sky of ceaseless grey. London had always been a place of transit to him, a city he spent a few days on his way somewhere else. He'd never stayed long enough for it ever to feel familiar.

As they neared the gallery, what he felt wasn't so much a sense of anticipation as a sense of dread. His body grew stiff with the awareness of what could go wrong; bad thoughts clung to him like tar.

He wasn't entirely sure why he did this to himself. Did he think people would only like him if he was bright and shiny and lit by success?

From his pocket, his phone gave off two quick pings. Who could be messaging him now? His thoughts rushed towards Dom, but instead it was his mother. *Good luck! Love, Mum.* In all of this, no matter what bad decisions he'd made, it helped to know she loved him.

●

The day before, Andrew had arrived at the London gallery, where he'd met Marten Smythe for the first time. His body didn't match the authority of his voice; he was a short dumpy man with a cropped, grey beard. He had a small, lipless mouth like an animal that only eats meat. Andrew knew immediately what sort of person Marten Smythe was: the type who crowds around success and who only wants to be around things that glow.

He had the USB stick with Phoebe's photos on it in the pocket of the jacket he was wearing. He had never made up his mind about whether to send it over. But it didn't matter now; he had decided that he didn't want to exhibit the photos of Phoebe. He felt sure of it and, as he shook Marten Smythe's hand, he knew that he had made the right decision.

'How was your flight?' Marten Smythe said.

'The flight was fine. The hardest part is the jet lag.'

'I'm sure it is. How far behind is Sydney?'

'It's ahead, by eight hours.'

Marten Smythe cleared his throat. 'Well, I'm not sure if there's been some hitch, but we still haven't received the high-resolution images of the girl with the face. We'll need those now, or I'm afraid we won't be able to proceed with the show.' His words sounded moderate, considering the threat they implied.

'Yes,' he replied. He would be strong. He wouldn't be pressured into doing something he didn't want to do. He would protect Phoebe's image. He would do the right thing and he would not bend to this man's will.

'Have you brought them with you? We really need them today, tomorrow will be too late. We need to have them printed.'

'Yes,' he said. 'Yes' seemed to be the only word he was capable of saying. 'I'm sorry, I got a bit busy.' He fiddled with the USB stick in his pocket.

Marten looked over to the office at the back of the gallery where a woman was sitting behind glass. The two of them exchanged a look that implied they had discussed this beforehand.

'If you give them to me now, we can arrange the printing for this afternoon. We have someone on standby at the printers.'

'Yes.' He stood still for a few more moments. Marten Smythe's eyebrows twitched. Andrew reached into the pocket of his jacket. In his head, he was telling himself that he had done enough. He had given them ten photographs that were already hanging in the gallery. They didn't need the photographs of Phoebe as well.

'I assume you have the files with you?' Marten Smythe had his hand held out.

'Yes,' he said.

Andrew couldn't help it. The way he had lived his life, his art had always come first. He had pursued it at the expense of everything else. He dropped the USB stick into Marten Smythe's plump hand.

•

The opening was already underway when he arrived that night at the gallery. He walked in and the room was full. There were more people than he expected and he stood on the threshold for a moment, wondering whether there was any way for him to avoid entering the room. The space was split across two levels and the walls were impossibly white. He stepped forward and forgot how loudly people spoke at openings, loud enough for their conversations to be overheard, and walking into the room he passed through several layers of sound.

Moving to the table of drinks he picked up and drank a glass of water, the sudden coldness of it making his throat seize. As he drank, he allowed his eyes to move around the room. The feeling he got when he saw the photos of Phoebe was lofty, of the floor moving away from underneath him. It wasn't very often that he permitted himself to feel proud of his own work.

Most of the photographs in this exhibition were portraits of people who appealed to him in some way. A man who'd worked for thirty years as a ferry driver, his face an escarpment of lines.

Marten Smythe walked towards him, accompanied by a man wearing a dark grey suit. Andrew couldn't stop staring at the man's tie, a very tight knot at the base of his throat. He had crumbs down the front of his shirt, the remnants of dismantled hors d'oeuvres. He wiped his hand on a paper napkin before he shook Andrew's hand.

It was always this way at openings: the lights shone too brightly in order to illuminate the work, but they made the people around them look too visible, their features grotesque. Marten introduced them; the man had already bought one of the photographs of Phoebe.

'Congratulations,' the man said, regarding him distantly. Marten moved away from them to speak to someone else.

'Thanks,' he said and smiled, but his smile felt painted onto his face.

'Where did you find the girl?'

The girl, he thought. He had done this to Phoebe, made her into an object. Some people would look at the photo he had taken of her and all they would see was what was wrong with her face.

The woman who worked at the gallery walked towards him with a glass of champagne. She was wearing a grey woollen dress, a soft sort of wool that made him want to rub his face against it. She squeezed his arm as though she knew him and left him to talk to the man in the tight suit alone.

'I actually found her at a school in Sydney near where I grew up,' he said.

'Well, the photos of her are very moving,' the man said, stepping backwards, drifting from him into the crowd.

The room seemed to have filled with even more people, which made him nervous. He had the sudden urge to leave, to step out into the cool air, hail a cab and allow it to whisk him away. His name was everywhere in the room, beside every photograph and all around him everyone was talking about his work, but still he didn't feel he was anywhere he belonged.

The woman who worked at the gallery moved from a conversation she was having behind him and stood by his side.

'You must be very happy with the result?' she said, looking up at him, stretching her neck and tilting her head upwards, like someone peering out from under an awning. Seeing this sudden vulnerability about her, he was reminded of Phoebe.

He looked into his drink and nodded.

'I guess it might also be quite confronting,' she said.

'Yes, I'm sorry. I'm not very good at this,' he said. Sometimes he felt he spent his life apologising.

'The photos of that girl, they really are something, though I guess you must have known that already?'

He looked at Phoebe's face on the bare white wall. 'I knew I had something,' he said. What was it he knew he had? In Phoebe he had seen something of himself and, by taking her photograph, he had preserved it.

'I like her a lot. Her name is Phoebe. She's interested in photography herself,' he said and the woman nodded.

More people were introduced to him and he spoke to them. They said kind things and he tried to respond graciously. After eight, the crowd started to disperse. He reassured himself that all the people around him would soon be gone and he could excuse himself for the night. But, then, where would he go? Retreat to his hotel room where the air was cool and all the sounds were muted? It was an empty room. A room he would depart from without leaving any trace of himself.

Around him, red dots were lined up beside his photographs, small red stepping stones creeping up the walls, and he knew he'd sold more prints than he'd ever sold before at an opening. But the thought jerked around inside him, like a small metal pinball. It meant nothing to him without Dom.

He had talked himself hoarse and now there was nobody left to talk to. The room was almost empty. He didn't want to be there, but he didn't want to be alone.

What was this feeling? He could only count this night as a success, but why did he feel he was standing on the water's edge with the tide pulling away from him?

Only the gallery staff remained and they had started packing away the tables and chairs around him. They moved quietly and swiftly, in a hurry for the night to be over. Marten Smythe was seeing the last guests down the stairs. It was a night that did not belong to them. Why did he put himself through this? For these fleeting moments of glory, after which everyone went back to their own lives and he was left to himself? He longed to speak to Dom.

He walked to a wall and looked up at one of his photographs: a woman whose lips didn't quite meet when her mouth was closed. He'd already sold three prints. It had taken him years and years of work, gradually learning how to take a photograph like that, with hours and hours of practice to perfect his technique and passing through every disappointment, every rejection, in order to come through the other side. The only thing that mattered to him was that he could find a way to keep doing this.

The woman from the gallery walked towards him. 'Should I call you a taxi?'

He nodded. He couldn't avoid it any longer. There was no reason for him to stay. She helped him down the stairs, her arm under his, and out to the cab, like he was a very old man being assisted to his last chair.

•

The taxi stopped outside his hotel, but he didn't go in. He walked instead to the Thames, navigating by some instinct his body had to find its way to water. The air outside was frigid and dry. When he reached the Thames, he walked along beside it, the water a dark and listless void. It was still light, although the sun had set, the city lights illuminated the night sky. A jogger wearing white paced towards him and offered a nod as he passed. Andrew looked at his watch. It was after ten. He wondered what such an existence was like, working hours so long you had to squeeze these ordinary activities into the corners of your life. That was one way to live and he had chosen another and he couldn't even say that one was preferable to the other, but at least he lived with the choice he had made.

On the opposite side of the river, Westminster was rimmed with light, its stony walls seamed and ornate. Ahead of him, the London Eye loomed, small capsules on a round wheel, shimmering and still. On the water a boat glided by, silent and sparkling with light. These were all photographs to him; pictures from postcards. But he understood now that photographs were a necessity to him, that every photograph he took was a protest against the type of silence Kirsten had taken to her grave.

•

That night, he slept better than he had expected to, a sleep that was thick and dark as though unfolding behind

296

a heavy curtain. When he woke, he realised it was almost eleven in the morning. He stood and opened the curtains; light flooded in. Cool, creamy European light. The light he loved to take photographs in.

He showered and went downstairs for breakfast, and when he entered his room again the telephone was ringing.

'Hello?'

'Andrew?' It was Marten Smythe. 'We were worried you might have left the country already,' he said. Andrew couldn't tell whether or not he was joking. 'You weren't answering your mobile.'

He picked up his phone from the bedside table; the screen was blank. 'Sorry,' he said. 'The battery must be flat.'

'Never mind,' Marten said. 'Have you seen the paper today?'

'No,' he said, wondering whether there had been some sudden catastrophe he hadn't heard about, a cyclone or tsunami on the other side of the world. Perhaps Marten wanted to warn him of it in case he was heading to the airport.

'There's a great review in *The Guardian*,' Marten said.

'Oh, okay.' He looked at his unmade bed as he spoke and felt a sudden urgent need to straighten it. He tugged the sheet up over the pillow as Marten read from the review. He listened, but he couldn't make sense of the words.

'I don't want to talk it up, but sales are strong, especially the one of the girl. I think we're going to sell every edition before the week is out,' Marten Smythe said before he ended the call.

Andrew went downstairs and asked for a paper.

'Which one, sir?' a young man with red hair said. Even his eyelashes were orange.

'*The Guardian*, if you have it.'

'Certainly,' he said and disappeared, reappearing with the folded paper.

Andrew read the review on the way back to his room. The photograph of Phoebe had been printed with the review and seeing it there shocked him; to see it on a gallery wall was one thing, but to see it in a newspaper meant it was available for all the world to see. It was a whole new level of exposure and he felt he had to show this to Pippa and Phoebe.

He read the review through. There were two sentences he read over again.

Spruce's subjects are flawed, but the broken faces that dominate his work are in their own way perfect. He gives his subjects careful attention, assiduously rendering each face. When you finally turn away from his photographs, it is conventional beauty that starts to seem strange.

It was true that the flaws were what he loved. He saw the flaws around him, in Dom, in his mother, in Phoebe, in Pippa and even in Kirsten, and he felt he was somewhere he belonged. To him there was more honesty in broken things than in things that looked shiny and new.

He took a photo of the article on his phone and sent

it to Pippa by email. He felt he had to own up to what he'd done.

He decided he'd go to the airport and see if he could take an earlier flight to Berlin, not really thinking beyond the fact that he wasn't prepared to wait any longer. He packed his suitcase so quickly that, as he took the tube to Heathrow, he was worried he might have left something behind. The stations as they slipped past sounded familiar: Leicester Square, Piccadilly Circus, Knightsbridge, names that sounded miniature and playful, like words that had been taken from a children's verse. It was after four and, around him, the other passengers were silent. They were commuters, dumbstruck from their day at work.

At the airport, he wheeled his bag to the sales desk, where he asked whether there were any flights to Berlin. There was one seat available on the next flight and he pushed his credit card across the counter. By the time he held the boarding pass in his hand, all he could think of was Dom.

30

He boarded the plane and sat in his seat by the window, watching as the bags were loaded below, impatient to take off. Taking the magazine from the seat pocket, he flicked through the slippery pages containing advertisements for luxury goods. People felt their richest when they travelled. He looked at the photos designed to seduce. He was glad he had freed himself from having to take pictures like this, telling small but inviting lies about the world.

As the plane lifted from the ground, he felt a sudden lightness, as though he was now, after weeks of procrastinating, on his way to solving all his problems. Optimism flooded through him like warm mead.

A little less than two hours later, the plane was circling over Berlin. He could just make out the cranes, yellow and orange struts perched next to buildings. It was a city permanently under construction, building and rebuilding itself, always conscious of the ruins from which it had come. From above, the Spree, silver in the sunlight, sliced through Berlin like a corrugated blade.

He retrieved his baggage then boarded a bus to the city centre. There was something comforting about moving through streets he knew and the familiar voices around him.

Instead of going straight to their apartment, he got off at Alexanderplatz and walked through Mitte, seeking out the familiarity of the streets there. He wanted to visit his studio first, the place where he'd spent most of his time in Berlin. He wanted to regain that sense of belonging he'd had before he left. How fleeting the feeling was; it came and, the moment he got used to it, he lost it again. Around him, Berlin was a patchwork of ugliness and beauty, a city that had survived a terrible history and had become something different and good. He loved this broken city.

When he reached the Spree he looked down at the water, which was dark and still. The metal rail along the edge felt frozen cold. He couldn't imagine wanting to submit to that darkness, the way Kirsten had submerged herself in the lake. He started walking towards his studio and on his way a group of young Australian girls with long hair passed him and their easy accent broke his concentration.

He walked through the front door and up one flight of stairs. He could never reconcile the grey exterior of the building and its sharp, definite lines, with the expansive spaces inside. The rooms in the building were big, cavernous and cool, ideal for studios. When he worked there, he liked being able to hear the movement of other people in the rooms above and beside his studio. He often thought when he was there of bees in a hive, working separately but together, towards a common purpose.

He unlocked his studio and the room was as empty as he'd left it. As he looked around he saw it contained no trace of him. He came here each day, he laboured, agonised over photographs or ideas he had for them. He failed constantly and he hated himself for it. And then, each night, he returned home to Dom. Her love gave him permission to fail.

His phone rang.

'Hello?'

'Andrew? It's Pippa.' He felt suddenly nervous, worried that she'd be angry at him for allowing Phoebe's image to be printed in a newspaper. 'I got your email.'

'The review?'

'Yes. Phoebe was impressed too. It sounds like the exhibition was a success?' There was a sudden quavering in her voice.

'Yes, I suppose it was.' He shut the door of his studio and walked out into the shadowy hall.

'Aren't you happy?'

'Happy? I don't know if that's the right word. Maybe more like relieved.' There were old glazed tiles lining the walls around him, a pattern of creams and a crimson so dark it might have been drawn from blood.

'Yes, I think I know what you mean.'

'You weren't upset, then?'

'About what?'

'That they put Phoebe's photo in the paper?'

'I suppose I was aware something like that might happen.'

He sighed. 'I didn't tell you, but I was thinking about not exhibiting Phoebe's photographs at all. In the end, though, I felt I had to go through with it.'

'I'm glad you did. The photos are striking. Sometimes when I look at them I think it doesn't even look like Phoebe at all.'

'I guess. I don't know.' He said his next words without really formulating them; they were words he had been thinking around. 'I used to think photographs were my way of speaking.' He wasn't sure why he was telling her this; for some reason he thought she'd understand.

'Your photographs are a beautiful language.'

'I thought photography could be everything I needed. But they are no substitute for conversation. Or laughing. Or touch.'

'I suppose not.'

There was a pause. Neither of them spoke, but there was no discomfort in their silence.

'Phoebe's here. Would you like to speak to her quickly?

'Sure,' he said, switching the phone to his other ear.

'Hello?' she said, as though the word were a question.

'Hi, Phoebe. How are you?'

'I'm good. My photograph was in the paper.' She sounded much younger on the phone than she did in person.

'It was, I'm sorry. I didn't know that would happen.'

'I don't mind. I like the photo.' She was quiet for a moment. 'I've been using the camera you gave me. Mostly I've been taking photos of plants. I really like leaves, the under-side with all the veins.'

'Leaves? I'm not sure I've ever photographed a leaf.'

'I think I understand why you take photos now.'

'Oh yeah?'

'Like the photograph of me. I'll never be like that again, will I? I'll always be changing,' she said.

'Yes, you will.'

'Because I'm living and it's not. I like the camera, but maybe I won't be a photographer when I grow up. Maybe I'll be something else instead.'

'What sort of thing?'

'Still something like what you do. Something that lets me say what I feel,' she said, loudly and clearly.

He closed his eyes and smiled, looking at the ceiling where watermarks had gathered in unusual shapes.

When they were finished talking he stood up and

moved towards his old Rolleiflex, still sitting there on the shelf. He picked it up and it felt metallic, the surface rough. The camera was a box of mystery given to him by his father that he hadn't been able to put down since.

Speaking to Pippa and Phoebe he understood he'd caused no permanent harm. Maybe he'd even in some way helped.

•

He took the U-Bahn to Kottbusser Tor and walked the familiar path to their apartment, his suitcase bumping along the grooves in the cement as he pulled it behind him. *Thud, thud, thud*, it sounded at regular intervals, like a measuring wheel. He'd walked this street so often he had the feeling that he was doing nothing unusual; he was returning home after a day's work and Dom would be as happy to see him as she always had been.

He crossed the street, walking on a diagonal. Since he'd been there last, the earth had tilted on its axis, moving back towards the sun. A feeling rose in him, a good feeling, a warm one. Such happiness in these moments before he had suffered disappointment, such bliss when all he had at his disposal was hope.

Not far away, the train thudded over its elevated track, the racket of metal and bolts that held it together. Along the side of the apartment building he saw graffiti, large swollen letters in green and silver, painted there in the black of night and now catching the last light of the day. What would Dom say to him now? Would she allow him to resume their love?

He buzzed the apartment instead of using his key. The noise was sudden and crude. Through the intercom he heard a voice, but one so far away it sounded like the trace of a voice, carried off by the wind.

'Dom?'

He thought he heard his name. The door clicked open when he pushed it.

He stood at the bottom of the stairs, unsure he could make it all the way to the top with his heavy suitcase. He negotiated the first flight of stairs and rested on the landing with his suitcase at his feet.

It was peaceful in the stairwell. He always enjoyed standing there, in this hall of doors. The winter light through the glass was watery. It filled the stairwell with ambient light. The branches on the trees outside cast spidery shadows on a wall. He felt suddenly alert. He was assessing the room for light, he realised. It was his automatic reaction to the world, to decide whether it would make a good photograph.

He looked up through the staircase towards his own door. There was light seeping out beneath it. It was faint but warm; it was the light they lived by. He took his suitcase in his hand and kept moving towards it.

Acknowledgements

This novel was completed as my creative project for a Doctorate of Creative Arts at the Writing & Society Research Centre, Western Sydney University. It has been one of my life's great privileges to work under the supervision of Gail Jones, whose insight, curiosity and unique intelligence have been an inspiration. Thank you also to Ivor Indyk for his prescient feedback on earlier versions of this manuscript in his usual, direct manner.

I'm also grateful to Rob Spillman whose thoughtful comments on an early version of the book helped me to find the novel's shape.

Thank you to Jane Palfreyman for believing in me and in this manuscript from an early stage and staying patiently with me through its many revisions. I'm also indebted to the editorial rigour of Ali Lavau.

Thank you to my dear friend Petrina Hicks who allowed me to observe one of her photo shoots and for her beautiful and poetic images.

To my writing friends, Fleur Beaupert, Brooke Robinson, Peggy Frew, Meg Mundell and Tegan Bennett-Daylight who offered kind and supportive words at difficult times. I'm grateful to both Peggy and Mireille Juchau for their generous words about this novel.

This novel was written with the support of a grant from the Copyright Agency Limited's Cultural Fund, which I used to undertake a residency at Can Serrat in Barcelona, Spain. Part of the novel was also written during a residency in Japan undertaken as part of University of Melbourne's Asialink Programme with the support of the Australia Council for the Arts and the Japan-Australia Foundation.

Special thanks to Julien Klettenberg, whose love and support are written into every page.